# Poor Man's Weapon

# Poor Man's Weapon

## David Drury

**VANTAGE PRESS**
New York

Published by Vantage Press, Inc.
516 West 34th Street, New York, New York 10001

Manufactured in the United States of America
ISBN: 0-533-12639-8

Library of Congress Catalog Card No.: 97-91320

0 9 8 7 6 5 4 3 2 1

To Aggie, always

# Poor Man's Weapon

# ONE

*In Country, north of Saigon, South Vietnam, November 1968*

Corporal Tommy Napoli sat in the shade with the six members of his squad, sipping Cokes, smoking cigarettes, and watching critically as the lanky marine second lieutenant walked briskly across the airfield tarmac.

Napoli was barechested, exposing a heavily tanned, muscular build on a short frame. The others wore either T-shirts or unbuttoned blouses with their fatigue trousers and boots. Including Napoli, four were whites, three were blacks. None was over age nineteen. All were sweating profusely under a clear, midday sun.

"So here comes our new shavetail," Napoli said, squinting through jet-black eyes that matched his bushy eyebrows and short-cropped hair. "Captain says he's quite the jock. All-American miler out of Stanford. From here it looks like he could beat a gazelle."

"Damn!" Oscar Riley, a tall, powerfully built black private said. "Means if he bugs out, he'll leave me in the dust and I'll be the one to get caught."

"Anyone could outrun you, lard ass," white Private Noobie Girard gibed.

"Watch your sassy mouth, honkey, lest I scrub your scrawny hide with sand fleas."

Giggling at his remark, Riley turned to Napoli.

"Think we oughta cover up, Nap?" he asked.

1

Napoli considered, then answered, "No point in takin' chances. He could be gung ho. Everybody square away."

The seven marines stood, put on or buttoned their field blouses, adjusted their caps, and came to attention, Napoli in front.

Napoli rendered the sole salute and greeted, "Afternoon, Lieutenant. Corporal Tomas Napoli, at your service."

The salute was returned, crisply.

"Good afternoon, Corporal, fellas. My name's McNeill, John McNeill. Let's sit a spell and go through the traps." Pointing to hundreds of fifty-five-gallon drums painted in various vivid colors, he continued, "I understand you're all new to this agent business."

"That's right, Lieutenant," Napoli replied as the others nodded in agreement. "We were pulled from a line company just two days ago. Don't know from nothin' about that stuff, technically speakin'."

"Well," McNeill said, removing his cap, which showed a sweaty brow under the blondest hair Napoli had ever seen, "if you were in country with a line outfit, you know about CS, or tear gas. You may've lobbed some of it into tunnels or bunkers to flush out Viet Cong. And if you've been around any length of time, you've probably seen the effects of some of our airplane spraying."

The seven nodded.

"Well," McNeill continued, "the official line is that CS is a non-fatal weapon, used as much in defense as in offense. Of course, if you happen to pitch a few into a confined space, like a cave or bunker, the occupants will probably wind up dead as doornails."

Corporal Napoli and the privates smiled knowingly.

"Incidentally," McNeill said, "if you guys would like to shed your jackets, be my guests. And smoke 'em if you got 'em."

As the men quickly removed their tops and lit up, McNeill resumed, "As for what's in the colored barrels, President Kennedy authorized their use late in sixty-one, under the buzz word Operation Ranch Hand. Its objective is to deny the enemy food and cover. They've caused a stink back home. You may've read or heard about those five thousand scientists who petitioned last year to end our use of CS and these other things in the barrels. In other words, we say they're non-lethal and those scientists said bull shit.

"Anyway, we're still using them by the millions of gallons. Chemicals in the blue barrels are meant to kill rice plants, those in the white barrels are designed to kill trees, and the ones in purple and orange contain a mixture of two chemicals that are used to kill the leaves of trees and shrubs."

"Lieutenant," Napoli said, raising his hand.

"Yes, Corporal."

"Meanin' no disrespect, sir, but the last CO we had said them agents ain't worth the powder to blow 'em to hell. He said the Charleys are still gettin' all the grub they need and that, sometimes, shreddin' all them plants and bushes makes it easier for 'em to ambush us."

McNeill grinned and replied, "Ours not wonder why, fellas. The reality is we're going to keep splattering the stuff around until we're told otherwise. You'll be taken through the hoops over the next couple of days. It's pretty much a no-brainer. Load the drums on those twin-engine transports, hose them up to the wing sprayers, and turn on the faucet when the pilot signals.

"Other than that, there's only one thing I want to impress on each of you, speaking as a guy who majored in chemistry. Regardless what you may be told in your orientation, I want you to be very careful with all of these agents.

If you're anywhere near them, wear your gas mask and handle them with gloves. I look at the situation quite fundamentally. I figured if that stuff can kill foliage, it could kill me. Enough said. There'll be a tech sergeant along pretty soon to fill you in on the work details. We'll probably be squirting Agent Orange, or whatever, in a couple days or so."

Dawn was just breaking as Second Lieutenant John McNeill arrived in a six-by truck at the side of the military transport plane, its twin propellers spinning in a warm-up. With him were Corporal Tommy Napoli and Privates Oscar Riley, Noobie Girard, and Boomer Wiley.

Riley, the only black in the crew, said to no one in particular as they clambered off the truck, "Y'know, I was only eleven years old when they started squirtin' this agent shit on Nam. Now I'm eighteen. Doesn't seem possible we could still be dickin' around this hole that long."

"Ain't no skin off your butt, Oscar," red-haired Noobie Girard said, with a laugh that showed off perfect teeth and deep blue eyes. "C'mon, gimme a hand with these flak jackets."

"My God, how many jackets are you guys tossing in there?" Lieutenant McNeill asked.

"Well, it's like this, sir," Boomer Wiley replied from a face festooned with freckles, as he easily held four bulky jackets in his powerful arms. "The gunny said the biggest hazard we'll face is sniper fire comin' in through the bottom of this crate. So, if wanna protect the family jewels," Boomer continued as he dropped a set of jackets and grabbed his crotch, "you better be standin' on somethin' tougher than boot leather, know what I mean, Lieutenant?"

McNeill shook his head, smiling, and addressed Corporal Napoli, "Nap, get them on board. I'm going to go up front and pay our respects to the pilots."

4

McNeill eased himself past a maze of orange barrels, poked his head into the cockpit, and introduced himself. The pilot was short and broad shouldered, with very black stubble on a decidedly tough-looking face. His insignia indicated his rank of first lieutenant. "Glad to meet you, Mac. I'm Pug DeGrazia. My co-pilot, Gino Torelli. As you can see, I'm the handsome one."

Second Lieutenant Torelli looked like he'd just stepped off the set as the drop-dead handsomest leading man in Hollywood, about six feet two with flashing dark eyes, brilliant black hair, and a smile that could melt the South Pole. Grinning as he reached for McNeill's hand, he said, gesturing at DeGrazia, "He calls himself Pug, but he dropped the l. It's really Plug, as in plug ugly. Say, didn't you run for Stanford, in the mile?"

When McNeill nodded, Gino said, "I thought so. You were good, real good. I ran for USC, but I wasn't in your league."

"Sorry, girls," DeGrazia interrupted, "gotta break up your love fest. Can't keep Charley waiting."

They were airborne and leveled off at one thousand feet. Below was a carpet of uninterrupted green. Off to the left about a quarter mile was pale blue water.

Lieutenant McNeill had checked his crew to satisfy himself that hoses and drums were properly connected, gas masks and gloves were on, the absolute minimum amount of flesh was exposed, and that all were familiar with the location of life preservers and inflatable rafts. There were no parachutes because of the low elevation of the flight pattern.

The plane descended sharply, leveled off again, and then the cabin light signaled. Napoli and the private quickly opened their assigned valves, releasing streams of Agent Orange from both sides of the transport.

All watched as the billowing streams floated down toward the thick jungle foliage.

Seconds later bullets began ripping through the bottom of the aircraft. The plane was dropping sharply to the left, shuddering violently as it descended.

McNeill struggled toward the cockpit. What he saw sickened then terrified him. Torelli was soaked in blood, his eyes open, obviously dead. DeGrazia's trousers were bloodied, but he was conscious, in great pain, and on the threshold of trauma.

"Pug," McNeill shouted over the noise of the faltering engine, "I'll help you handle the controls, but we've got to head for water. We don't stand a chance landing on all those trees."

The pilot nodded, grimaced, cut the throttle, and motioned McNeill to help pull the shaking controls up and then to the left, as the damaged engine burst into flames.

Minus power, they kept dropping ever closer to the tree tops.

With all his strength, McNeill pulled back on the controls from behind DeGrazia's back. The tail dropped. A beach appeared. The pilot passed out. In less than minutes, they had cleared the last tree and were belly-landing in the sea. Cool water gushed in.

McNeill released the unconscious pilot's harness and dragged him through the cockpit door. Riley, Girard, and Wiley had made it to the outside, but Corporal Napoli, horrified as the water climbed up his waist, screamed "I can't swim, Lieutenant. I can't swim!"

McNeill reached up and pulled from the overhead lacing a couple of life preservers. He skimmed one to Napoli and put the other around DeGrazia. The water was now up to his mouth.

Napoli ducked through the door opening, in his desperation almost crushing the preserver.

McNeill followed, pushing DeGrazia's head under water so they could clear the door top. As he did so, his left leg was caught by a piece of jagged metal, cutting him to the bone from knee to ankle. He cried out, wrenched himself loose, and cleared the plane with his comatose burden. The plane disappeared instantly under the lapping waves.

Looking around, McNeill saw that the three privates had managed to scramble onto one of the plane's four-man inflatable rafts and were paddling toward him. Napoli was only a few yards away, still wide eyed with terror.

When the raft was alongside, McNeill ordered those aboard to lift the pilot on and apply a belt tourniquet, and said, "Nap, and I will stay in the water, hanging onto the side ropes. The current's taking us in. Paddle us away from land. Charley's in there waiting to kill us. We've got to hang out here until it's dark. And, Nap, for God's sake, quit squeezing that Mae West and put it on."

The words were scarcely out of his mouth when a muffled thumping sound was heard, followed by the distant report of a rifle. The center of Noobie Girard's chest seemed to explode, spewing blood and matter all over the raft.

"He got it in the back, Lieutenant," Private Boomer Wiley reported, as more bullets plinked around them. "He bought the farm, sir. Whadda we do?"

"Throw him overboard," McNeill commanded, "and keep paddling away from land. Nap, climb up there."

As he was tossing up the life preserver he had failed to put on, Corporal Napoli screamed as a bullet chopped through his right shoulder. He flailed his legs and left arm, but went under almost immediately.

McNeill vomited. The pain in his left leg was excruciating, and he was losing his crew one man at a time.

"Keep paddling," he yelled. "I'm going after Nap."

McNeill ducked under the water and saw nothing. He allowed his body to drift with the inbound current, to the spot he estimated Nap had taken the hit, and again ducked under. He saw Nap's listless body roughly three feet blow. Lungs afire, he grasped the unconscious corporal and yanked him to the surface.

Holding his face up under the chin, the lieutenant did a frantic side stroke toward the raft, which had stopped twenty yards away, or as soon as Riley and Wiley saw the pair surface.

"Soon as you get him in, Boomer, use mouth-to-mouth," McNeill ordered. "I'll stay in and swim-push while Oscar paddles. Nap'll probably need a tourniquet."

The enemy fire continued slapping into the waves, but the slowly increasing distance took a merciful toll on marksmanship.

Boomer's resuscitative efforts proved successful. Nap threw up violently.

"He's comin' round, Lieutenant," Boomer Wiley reported. "I put a tourniquet around his arm and shoulder. He took a tough one."

"Music to my ears," McNeill said. "Now ease up on the tourniquet on the pilot. Let a little blood flow to restore circulation, then tighten it again."

"Then what, Lieutenant?" Oscar Riley asked in a voice trying to mask despair.

Before McNeill could answer with what he knew would be a lie of false hope, he heard the unmistakable whump-whump-whump of two helicopters. The base had obviously become concerned when the Agent Orange plane had not reported back on its estimated time of arrival.

One chopper whooshed directly overhead and passed them, its merciless machine guns tearing into the jungle bordering the beach. Then it doubled back, dropping canisters of napalm, incinerating hundreds of yards of foliage and the Charleys lurking within.

The other helicopter hovered fifty feet over the raft and lowered a crane from its belly.

"Cinch Lieutenant DeGrazia to the hook," McNeill said, "then Nap, then Oscar. You'll go next, Boomer. I'll bring up the rear."

"But you're wounded, Lieutenant," Oscar Riley protested.

"Don't argue. Do it!"

A week later, lying in his Saigon military hospital bed, his wounded leg swathed in gauze and elevated by a ceiling wire, John McNeill opened two envelopes.

The first was colorfully emblazoned with the Marine Corps emblem, with a penned arrow extending to one side. It read, "You saved my hide on the Marine Corps birthday, November 10, 1968. I'll never forget that date and what you done. I owe you BIG TIME! Tommy Napoli."

The other read: "You're one helluva *Marine*. 'Thanks' seems awfully inadequate, but I can't imagine anything else that would fit the bill. Semper fi. Pug DeGrazia."

# TWO

President Fidel Castro, dressed in military fatigues, scratched his beard, bit hard on his cigar, placed his hands behind his back, and stared silently at the scene several hundred yards below.

There, in pastoral splendor, lay perhaps five thousand pigs, many apparently dead, others in what appeared to be the final throes of fatal agony.

He turned slowly to appraise the retinue that had followed him. It included a half-dozen men in civilian dress, roughly a dozen others in high-ranking military attire, and fifty muscular and heavily armed soldiers.

With studied calmness, Castro looked at one in the gathering and said, "Well, Doctor Camerra, what?"

The doctor, a short, slim man, glanced to his sides, walked the several paces separating him from his towering inquisitor, and whispered, "African swine fever, Mister President."

"And?" Castro asked softly.

"An apparent poisoning, similar to what occurred on the other side of the island."

"Your prescription?"

"Isolate the area, keep the affected inhabitants clear of the diseased, and slaughter all pigs within the vicinities, as many as a half million."

"Thank you. Do what you must," Castro said, nodding toward a bemedaled General Juan Juarez.

When he was at his side, Castro asked his swarthy aide, "Your guess?"

General Juarez smiled ruefully and answered, "Two widely separated spots suddenly afflicted with an uncommon animal virus. That would seem to eliminate any element of coincidence or chance. You'll recall I felt the same about the outbreaks of dengue fever that sickened three hundred fifty thousand of our people and ruined square kilometers of our tobacco and sugar cane crops. My guess? Then as now, I'd say it's the work of our good friends at the CIA."

"Your guess is probably as good as mine or any other's," Castro said, adding, "It makes me wonder if that pernicious gang has ever read the UN's report of a couple of years ago, the one on relative costs of large-scale military attacks on civilians. Remember?"

"Emphatically," the general replied. "With conventional weapons, the price was two thousand dollars per square kilometer, eight hundred dollars with a nuclear attack, six hundred dollars for nerve gas, and only a dollar per square kilometer if one used biological weapons."

Castro's chuckle brought a quizzical look from his general.

"I was thinking about the irony of that delightful movie with Alec Guinness, *The Mouse that Roared*," the president explained. "A tiny nation invades the United States for the purpose of surrendering and then receiving foreign aid. It was a brilliant little caper. They did it all on the cheap. I like the analogy, vis-à-vis the cost of biological weapons. Even the poorest nation can afford an arsenal that costs only a dollar per square kilometer, eh?"

# THREE

*The Iranian Desert Bordering Iraq, January 1984*

Inside the large air-conditioned tent, the dozen scientists comprising the United Nations fact-finding team listened attentively as Professor Takashi Isoru outlined the schedule for their first day on location.

Takashi, who was short, frail, and bent with age, was dressed like all the others, except one, in lightweight business suits. The only unusual element in their appearance was their hand-held gas masks.

The exception was the tall, trim American whose platinum-colored hair inspired the others to refer to him as the silver fox. He was Lieutenant Colonel John McNeill, United States Marine Corps, and his outfit was camouflage military fatigues.

Takashi had reviewed the group's formal charge, namely to determine the accuracy of Iran's complaint that Iraq was using poison gas against its soldiers and civilians. "Mercifully," he continued, "it should not take us long to examine the shells and shrapnel that have been acquired for us and to make our determination."

The listeners applauded, knowing they would soon be leaving their cool tent for an atmosphere hovering around one hundred ten degrees Fahrenheit. That grim fact prompted Takashi to indulge his curiosity.

"Colonel," he said as he approached the marine, "I couldn't help but notice you self-injecting. May I ask what for?"

"Anthrax vaccination," McNeill replied easily, looking at his little inquisitor through friendly gray eyes.

"And this uniform you're putting on in place of your fatigues. What a terrible burden in the heat we're soon to encounter. Would you please describe it for me?"

"I guess you could equate me with a guinea pig, Professor," McNeill answered, holding up his gas mask. "This thing holds two kinds of filters. One removes dangerous microorganisms, much like a sponge absorbs water. The other has activated charcoal to absorb chemical gas molecules, make them stick to the charcoal's surface instead of absorbing them.

"Under the two jackets and pants I'll be wearing," McNeill continued, "there's charcoal foam to trap toxic gases. Then there are the rubber gloves and overboots. The other stuff includes medicated towelettes, injectors for antidotes against nerve gas, and these adhesive-backed paper strips. If they're touched by a poisonous chemical, they turn red."

"Interesting," Takashi observed, bobbing his bald head. "None of us here thought about potential military defensive tactics. Your government obviously did."

"Oh, it's a bit more than that," McNeill said with a tinge of iciness. "One of these days, we might have to send troops to this region to secure our oil supply lines. This investigation provides a plausible pretext for my observations on that score. That aside, and perhaps your manifest doesn't reveal it, I also have a doctorate in chemistry from Stanford University, am a lecturer at the Naval War College in chemical and biological warfare, do the same stint for the Marine Corps Officers School in Quantico, Virginia, and am an adjunct professor at Georgetown University."

Takashi looked stunned. When he composed himself, his eyes shifting quickly to determine if anyone might be overhearing he asked, "Then I must assume you know my background?"

"Yep," McNeill said, "the whole magilla. You were among our prize catches at the end of World War II. You were comparable to the capturing of Werner Von Braun and his rocket-scientist goons in Germany. They got all the attention. You and your guys were into a dirtier end of the war business, but considered valuable nonetheless. You had the advantage of actually killing prisoners in chemical and biological experiments. Never mind that some of those prisoners were Americans. You also had years of experience between nineteen thirty-seven and forty-five in using poison gases against China's peasants and soldiers. Yours was the first documented case of germ warfare since the British peddled blankets taken from smallpox hospitals to American Indians more than a hundred years ago. Despite furious Soviet protests, you beat the war crime tribunals and were given the life of Riley at Fort Detrick, Maryland, where you had free rein to play with the most treacherous compounds on the face of the earth. Right?"

An extremely agitated Takashi responded, "Shall we proceed, Colonel McNeill?"

As expected, the heat was virtually unbearable. John McNeill made mental notes on how difficult it would be for a soldier to navigate in protective clothing that challenged his every movement. How could he move quickly in boots that weighed down the slightest exertion, or manipulate a rifle through rubber-gloved hands? And the damnable sand! It was like nothing he'd ever encountered.

Instead of granular particles as on a beach back home in the States, this desert's sand was more a dust or powder that could somehow find its way through successive layers of clothing.

The UN team probed the dozens of bombs, artillery shells, and pieces of shrapnel arrayed before it, taking samples for subsequent cultures and microscopic examination.

That phase completed, the inspectors were taken by small truck caravan over several miles of dust-filled road to an Iranian hospital. There they examined scores of alleged victims of poison warfare, in age ranging from toddlers to the very elderly. Each displayed body parts hideously scarred or blistering. Others were convulsing or suffocating.

Somberly and silently they trundled back to the trucks and retreated to the sanctuary of their air-conditioned tent. Hunched over their microscopes, they peered at one slide after another, then waited, uncertain as to what to do next.

Professor Takashi broke the impasse. "Would anyone care to venture his appraisal, gentlemen?"

The scientists glanced furtively at each other, but no one volunteered to be first to speak. Not, that is, until Lieutenant Colonel John McNeill, in T-shirt and fatigue pants, stood and cleared his throat.

"Far as I'm concerned," he said matter of factly, "I'm satisfied the evidence confirms the first use in history of nerve gas, with doses of mustard gas throw in for good measure. The nerve-gas culprit is tabun, developed in Germany near the end of World War II, and the predecessor of the even deadlier German-invented sarin and soman.

"The mustard gas would seem to account for the scarring and blisters. Tabun would seem to explain the wild, uncontrollable victim behavior. Its inhalation or absorption

through the skin blocks the enzyme action that stops trans-
mission of nerve impulses. Hence the frantic breathing and
eventual death."

Turning toward Takashi, McNeill smiled and added,
"Bet you spotted this right from the git go, eh, Professor?"

The UN inspection team report confirmed the use of
nerve and mustard gas by Iraq, in March, nineteen eighty-
four. Iraq went unpunished and continued use of the illegal
arms into nineteen eighty-eight.

# FOUR

Corbin Bates and Carter Urban relished the mystique surrounding their positions as clandestine operatives for the Central Intelligence Agency, as well as the virtually carte blanch perquisites that accompanied them.

Among the latter was the elegant breakfast they were now enjoying in one of Washington, D.C.'s poshest, the Madison Hotel, smack across the street from *Newsweek*, in the sweltering summer of nineteen eighty-nine.

By appearance alone, they fit in well with the distinguished clientele. Both were in their graying fifties, were impeccably and expensively dressed, had been in the Capital loop for almost thirty years, and could recognize most of the many political and media celebrities in the surrounding tables. Here, a gregarious Russian foreign minister and his bargain-hunting retinue, there, a nationally syndicated columnist extracting insider stuff from an obliging cabinet member.

Corbin Bates lifted a glass of tomato juice and said, "Here's to the blessings of air conditioning."

To which Carter Urban responded with a clinking of glasses, "I'll drink to that, and to Reagan-Bush."

"Amen," Bates said and continued, "Let's run through the traps again before the next appointment."

Urban, the subordinate, immediately took on a serious mien. "Right." Raising a hand and extending its index finger, he said, "Between nineteen sixty-two and sixty-seven,

Egypt smacks Yemen with mustard gas, killing and maiming thousands. The U.N. looks the other way."

Raising a second finger, he added, "In nineteen seventy-nine, our army confirms the use of commie mustard gas in Laos the year before. But that smart-ass, jarhead, John McNeill, and a gaggle of his chemistry boys claim the yellow rain was nothing more than bee excrement, for crissake. Again, the U.N. dawdles.

"Also in seventy-nine," raising a third finger, "there's an anthrax epidemic in Sverdlovsk. The Russians say it's due to contaminated meat. We know better. It happened in the vicinity of a germ warfare plant. They either had an accidental spill or were playing with delivery of a new toy."

Bates nodded, his sharp blue eyes darting in concentration.

Urban raised a fourth finger. "We jump ahead to nineteen eighty-seven. Libya squirts Chad with chemical gas. The U.N. says ho hum. Reagan says screw 'em all and dumps the chemical warfare production moratorium Nixon imposed eighteen years earlier.

"Good thing, too," Urban continued, "because Iraq kills five thousand Kurds with mustard gas a year later. Surprise, surprise, the U.N. sits on its hands."

Bates took a bite of his eggs Benedict, swirled his fork to pick up more of the delicious sauce, and sighed. "Not a pretty picture. Especially when you consider the potential in the Middle East. Iran, Syria, Israel, Libya, Ethiopia, Egypt, and Iraq comprise a full third of all the nations capable of producing chemical weapons."

Urban wiped his mouth with a napkin and waited patiently for his superior to mind rummage. Years of practice inculcated a pragmatic silence whenever a report seemed completed.

18

Bates nodded slowly, his preamble to a firm decision. "I'm going to make the rounds on The Hill, talk to some of our best cheerleaders, get them even more aboard on saying to hell with all of those useless anti-chemical and biological protocols. When push comes to shove, they're not worth the paper they're written on. There're simply no solid procedures for verifying complaints and then slapping violators down. Besides, it's too damned easy to loophole from ostensibly making defensive chemicals to making offensive ones. First, though, let's have that chat with Professor Takashi. I want to hear the latest on what our little Nip friend has been up to, and how we can best proceed under the circumstances."

Within an hour of the summoning phone call, Professor Takashi Isoru arrived in his white, chauffered limousine at the entrance of the Madison Hotel.

Agents Bates and Urban entered quickly and offered a curt greeting to the aged Japanese scientist, whose wide grin exposed heavily browned and snaggled teeth.

Bates gestured with a finger, indicating to the driver that he must raise the glass partition, which would preclude their being overheard. He then made a circling motion with his finger, instructing the chauffeur to drive around until ordered otherwise.

"On the way over from Maryland, I had to chuckle, gentlemen," the all-white clad Takashi said, "as I glanced at the capital's profusion of Japanese cherry trees."

Bates and Urban looked at each other with flat eyes that appeared to ask, so?

"In World War II," Takashi resumed, "they were suddenly referred to as Korean cherry trees. Times change as do the circumstances. They're now, again, Japanese trees. I enjoy such paradoxes."

Bates ignored the story, indicating not the slightest interest in a possible implication, and cut to his chase, "What do you have worth listening to?"

Takashi had anticipated the question on his drive from Fort Detrick and had pondered an adequate answer. He always strived to satisfy his clients and, with tens of billions of dollars at its disposal, the CIA represented the creme de la creme.

Takashi leaned his head back to assess the ceiling, folded bony hands over a short, bony knee, and began. "Since the early seventies, my colleagues and I have known how to combine the genetic materials of two different organisms. This splicing of a gene from organism into the genetic material of another, DNA, creates new life form with the characteristics of both organisms. We call it biotechnology or genetic engineering. Whatever, it is amenable to mass production. On one hand, it makes possible the relatively inexpensive development of insulin and various vaccines that would otherwise be in short supply. Also, we have the capability of altering a deadly but rare disease that could be cheaply mass-produced, as well as improving the survivability of microorganisms as they are fired from whatever source of delivery.

"We can strengthen germs to bypass vaccinated troops, increase their deadliness, and accelerate their impact to within hours instead of days. We can make toxic what is otherwise a harmless bacteria and change microbes to kill cattle and plants.

"And on the other hand?" Bates interrupted.

"On the other hand," Takashi continued, "as in anything of great consequence, there are the hazards associated with someone turning the tables on you."

"You take care of the offense. Let us worry about the defense," Bates said. "Can tests with this DNA stuff be simulated? Can it be tried out on, say, a large domestic populace without killing people?"

Takashi shrugged and smiled. "We've been using Americans and others as human guinea pigs since the postwar U.S.-Soviet chemical arms race. Before you and Agent Urban even joined the company. In the mid-fifties, the CIA tested mind-altering drugs on hundreds of unsuspecting people. At the same time, we tested along the Florida Gulf Coast, with the result that the number of whooping cough cases tripled.

"Between nineteen forty-nine and sixty-nine, millions of Americans in two hundred thirty areas were subject to simulant organisms. The army said they were harmless. Doctors who testified at Senate hearings took the opposite tack. Problem was, the army had failed to monitor the health impact."

"Where the hell are you going with all this?" Bates cut in irritably.

"I'm not absolutely certain simulant DNA tests are feasible," Takashi replied evenly. "It would be an interesting experiment, to say the least. Perhaps such could be tried on a limited basis, possibly with farm animals, later with humans. As always, your wish is my command."

Bates tapped on the window separator and ordered the driver to return to The Hill.

Addressing Takashi, Bates said, "Proceed full bore with a simulant test. Let me know the minute you're ready to give it a try."

Bates and Urban got out of the limousine and walked quickly away from it, neither bothering to wave a goodbye.

Takashi, eyes boring into the back of the chauffeur's head, demanded sharply, "Did you get it all?"

The driver held up a taped cassette, nodded, and smiled.

Takashi relaxed, returned the smile, and ordered, "Take me back to the lab."

# FIVE

The marines' base at Quantico, Virginia, in the midsummer of nineteen ninety-three was predictably but dismayingly hot, even at six o'clock in the morning. It was an atmosphere that would get progressively more oppressive with each passing hour, as it would in Washington, D.C., roughly fifty miles away, and at other marine installations along the Eastern seaboard, including Parris Island, Camp LeJeune, and Cherry Point.

Collectively, they helped account for the marines' assumption that, when they died, they went straight to heaven because they'd served their time in Hell.

That thought probably drifted in and out of the approximately thirty officers who jogged along rows of brick buildings and immaculate lawns on their daily five-mile run. From their marine-emblemed caps and sweatshirts to their full-length cotton trousers and combat boots, they displayed the maximum load of perspiration.

Most of the joggers were young lieutenants leavened with a couple of captains, a major, a lieutenant colonel, and two full bird colonels.

The daily morning running routine had begun with only the two colonels. The sight of the two "old men" had inspired emulation. Little by little, the joggers' ranks swelled to the current number. Depressingly for the young turks, the "old" colonels always led the parade, always finishing one, two at the huge flagpole that marked the finish.

Within a quarter mile of the pole, Colonel John McNeill winked to his close friend, Colonel Jake Coltrane, and raised and lowered his right arm in a pumping motion that signaled they were entering the final, all-out spurt.

Shouting "Semper fi!," they all dashed toward the finish.

Smiling, but in continued disbelief, the younger officers passed by the "old men," saluting and panting "Number One" as they proceeded by Colonel McNeill and "Number Two" as they went by Colonel Coltrane, who were breathing easily, as though they'd just taken a leisurely stroll.

"Tomorrow?" McNeill yelled.

"Tomorrow!" they chorused, many shaking their heads at the physical dominance of men old enough to be their fathers.

As they lathered up in the senior officers' showers, Jake Coltrane shook his curly salt-and-pepper hair, raised impressively muscled arms over a six-foot, trim body, and exulted, "Best part of the day. Y'know, John, if you dyed that steel gray mop of yours, you'd still look like you were on Stanford's track team."

McNeill smiled back. Without trying to flatter himself, there was an element of truth in what was just said. Despite his fifty-three years, John McNeill had the physique and unlined face of a superb athlete, as did Jake Coltrane. "Maybe I'll go Hollywood," he said, adding, "Got time for a bite?"

"Sure," Coltrane answered, "but tell me something, now that I'm looking at it. How long did it take to get over that knee-to-ankle scar you got in Nam?"

"I was lucky not to have been gimpy the rest of my life," McNeill said. "Got rescued before it could fester. Had a great surgeon and a phenomenal therapist. Most important, I had Julie every inch of the way."

McNeill made a sad, distracted pause. Recovering quickly, he said, "A few years of agony and I was ready for a second tour in country. Let's eat."

They sat at a table for two in the officers' glistening mess hall, with its spotless white cloths and heavy table ware. In deference to the humidity, both wore tieless khaki shirts, with three sharp creases down the backs.

Coltrane had eagles pinned to his collars and five colorful rows of ribbons. McNeill sported the eagles but no ribbons.

As they finished their grapefruit and started in on the dry cereal and milk, Coltrane said, "I see you're again tempting the commandant's wrath by not wearing your fruit salad. Man, I've got the rows, but they'd never match your Navy Cross, Silver Star, Bronze Star, and three Purple Hearts, to name just the top echelons."

McNeill replied, "As for the commandant's conniptions, frankly, Scarlett, I don't give a rat's ass. I'm in countdown for the big good-bye. What's he going to do, throw me in the brig, when I'm weeks away from retirement? As for displaying my toys, I'm not out to impress anybody. Actually, the older I get, the less enthralled I am by medals and the things we poor, obedient boobs do to get them."

"Kathy wants you over for dinner tonight," Coltrane said. "Can do?"

"Could but won't," McNeill answered. "Look, Jake, Kathy's a treasure and I really appreciate her empathy. But, like every other senior officer's lady I bump into, she wants to play matchmaker. Not play. I don't mean to trivialize. It's just that female impulse to mitigate emotional pain. It's in their genes.

"Ever since the DUI blindsided us coming back from D.C. eighteen months ago, I never dreamed I could survive without Julie. My heart atrophied. I was and am a one-woman guy. The only female companionship I want is my daughter Amy's. I'd've gone ape without her. God knows, I owe her a back order for all the time I spent away. So, I'm winding down the old career here and then heading for Montana and my little curly head."

"What the hell will an antsy pants like you do in those boondocks?" Coltrane asked.

"Whatever makes Amy happy. Fortunately, she's a full-fledged jock, so we'll get in plenty of licks hiking, running, hunting, canoeing, white-water rafting, and fishing. And, I've gotten some solid vibes back for a few teaching and lab positions, including the chemical plant where Amy's a lab go-fer. What have you got on for today? More boom, booms?"

"More boom, booms." Coltrane smiled. As McNeill was to military chemical and biological warfare, Coltrane was the military's icon in conventional explosives. "I'm wrapping up tests on stuff whose I.D. is even top secret. Makes the biggest bomb bang to date look like a wet fire-cracker. Couple pounds and it can make an eight-story building disappear. It's very malleable, like play dough, and just as harmless until touched off. Better yet, we've got a newly improved, non-metallic blasting cap that can be exploded with a battery-triggered detonator the size of a pen. You?"

"From here I go for my karate lesson with Gunny Taino," McNeill said, displaying thick calluses along the knife edges of his large hands. "It's a great workout and helps keep me from wallowing in self-pity.

"After that I'll put on one of my dog-and-pony shows for a gaggle of marine field-grade officers, some FBI guys, a few foreign military, and the inevitable CIA flunkies who shy away from being identified as such. They're always trying to keep tabs on me."

"Not one of their publicity flacks, are you?" Coltrane asked.

"Only when I catch them stepping out of line. Never cottoned to them. They've got far too much money and unsupervised power. Scary, really."

When they were outside, McNeill bent down to extract a pack of cigarettes with matches from inside a sock. He lit up.

Coltrane shook his head in mock dismay. "Thirty-four years of hellfire and brimstone against fags by the surgeon general, and you remain the stubborn infidel."

"You shouldn't trust generals of any persuasion, my boy. Don't you scan the editorial cartoons? Those guys are professional journalists. That's why they depict all generals as being overweight, arrogant, and stupid.

"Poor Julie tried for years to get me to kick the habit until, ever the pragmatist, she finally threw in the towel. Not Amy, though. Even as a tyke she'd circle my cigs half their length with a pen, indicating I shouldn't puff beyond those marks. Gradual withdrawal thingie. Even now she keeps sending me those smoke-no-more patches and chewing gum, along with magazine and newspaper articles, as well as tape cassettes, on how to forswear kissing Dame Nicotine. Poor kid. I'm incorrigible.

"Give my regrets and thanks to your lady. See you tomorrow, when my polluted lungs will leave yours well to the rear."

Quantico's lecture theater was large and filled to capacity with perceptive students, including a dozen women, dressed as military and civilian. Long red and opened drapes adorned large windows that allowed the nine A.M. sunshine into the cushioned-seat, air-conditioned environment.

A tall, distinguished-looking marine colonel approached the lectern at the elevated center stage, took from it a small corded microphone, slipped it around his neck, and announced, "My name is John McNeill. My job is to give you, in a series of lectures, an overview of chemical and biological weapons, an examination of the international protocols and conventions governing them, an update on the so-called state of the art of such weaponry and, within limits, the hoped-for defenses we've arranged against them. You're free to take notes if you wish, but I think you'll find they're unnecessary, what with the copious hand-outs you'll receive at the end of each session.

"I'll begin by capsulizing the historical context of chemical and biological weapons. It goes further back than many of you may have imagined. As far back as three thousand B.C., actually, when it was discovered that certain items added to fire could choke or sicken an enemy."

McNeill strolled easily back and forth across the stage as he continued. "In four thirty-two B.C., the fight between Greek states, known as the Peloponnesian War, unveiled the first flame-throwers. Bellows were pumped at the end of a pipe that propelled fire against wooden walls."

At a finger snap, a huge screen with a rear projector displayed a map of Greece, arrows pointing at Athens and Syracuse, and various products labeled pitch, sulfur, pine, and sawdust. "With a mix of these," McNeill said, pointing, "the boys from Syracuse found a concoction that could turn Athenian battering rams into kindling.

"But wait, there's more," McNeill said, "I'm just warming up."

His audience chuckled.

"In A.D., sixty-six," he resumed, "a clever cuss by the name of Callinicus—hey, that's alliterative—whipped these together," pointing to another screen projection that displayed elements labeled pitch, sulfur, quicklime, and naptha or petroleum obtained from pools. "The result came to be known as Greek Fire. With it, Byzantine Greeks were able to repulse attacks by Arabs and Russians at Constantinople.

"We'll have much more on the development and use of chemicals in war, but I'm going to leap frog into the biological stuff then skip merrily back.

"It wasn't until the nineteenth century that scientists could demonstrate that germs cause infectious diseases, that there were really such things as viruses, bacteria, and rickettsia. But long before that, observant warriors figured out that you could poison an enemy army by simply tossing a carcass or corpse into wells or other water sources.

"In thirteen forty-six A.D., the Tartars laid siege to what was then called Caffa, but which we now refer to as Feodosya, in Ukraine, on the east coast of the Black Sea. It was an untidy time. The Tartars became afflicted with plague and, rather than waste useful, diseased corpses, they hurled them into Caffa. The poor, predominately Italians within fled to Europe, bringing the plague with them, wiping out a quarter of the world's known population.

"We're talking really nasty consequences here, ladies and gentlemen. We've had too much attention focused on nuclear weapons, which are admittedly horrifying. But it's been at the expense of focusing honestly and realistically on a threat that is comparably horrifying, perhaps even worse. You think you can nuke 'em back to the Stone Age? They, including the poorest among our nations, can chem or germ us back to the same place, and beyond."

# SIX

Professor Takashi Isoru loved to putter in his high wood-fenced garden. It was a microcosm of the Japan he had been forced to leave many decades ago, with its plethora of imported shrubs and miniature trees, even a scaled-down copy of Mount Fuji, from whose sides rippled soothing waters that forked in rivulets that traversed his sunny oasis.

All matched the quiet remoteness of his lavish single-story, pagoda-style home in suburban Maryland, well removed from his laboratory at Fort Detrick.

Dressed in purple sandals and a white kimono with a purple sash, he walked inside his house to wash his hands and make a final appraisal in anticipation of an imminent tea ceremony. Takashi revered tea-ceremony masters as Americans idolized sports heroes. His shelves were lined with books in Japanese, which described in exhaustive detail a virtually uncountable number of tea ceremonies. The type, quantity, and arrangement of flowers had to be coordinated to perfection.

The same for the provision of slippers for the guests, as well as the mats, pillows, wall greetings, and tea cups.

As with the garden, Takashi's house looked like a wealthy Japanese transplant. Gleaming lacquered pots and bowls in predominant blacks and reds, varnished natural hardwood floors that sparkled, authentic pastel paintings of Oriental fishermen, a variety of pillows, and a one-hundred-gallon aquarium with multi-colored carp.

Satisfied, he called, "Akita."

The young woman appeared instantly, bowing and shuffling in half-steps silently across the floor. Quite young, she, too, was wearing a kimono, shimmering red silk with a white sash. The latter's chalky composition matched her heavily powdered face. Her jet-black hair was swept up all around in a huge bun accented by a red comb.

"Professor-sama?" she inquired anxiously.

"You are to be complimented. All is in readiness. When they arrive momentarily, escort them to the garden."

Akita bowed and backed herself out of the living room. Takashi returned to the garden and smelled the flowers.

"The time is at hand," he spoke softly, a half-smile on his lips and a determined glint in his rheumy eyes.

In moments, the servant came to him very deferentially and said, "They are here, Professor-sama."

CIA agents Corbin Bates and Carter Urban strode in with their usual imperious air. Takashi noticed immediately that neither had exchanged his street shoes for the slippers Akita had offered. He gestured them toward a circle of pillows, at the center of which was a colorful tea service, with napkins and appetizer bowls.

At Takashi's nod, Akita poured tea into the small cups and departed.

"What's all this hurry-up meeting business about?" Bates asked irritably, searching quickly around the garden. "And before you answer, I don't want to hear any specific reference to our respective agendas. If you must, use euphemisms. We'll get your drift."

Takashi calmly ignored the implication he'd arranged a taping of their conversation and said, "I am a very old man and in declining health. My doctor informs me I must seek a more commodious climate, albeit in your country. I have made arrangements to do so forthwith. This is my

31

formal notice to you that I am retiring and that I will leave your employ in two weeks."

Bates looked at Urban and chuckled, "Velly solly, perfesser, but you're in for the duration, the duration of your life, that is. You'd've been swinging from a yardarm in forty-five if we hadn't gotten to you instead of the Russkies. You've been well-paid, living it up like Paddy's pig, and we've got those tests to complete, remember?"

Takashi used his chopsticks expertly to pop a slender piece of raw fish and sauce into his mouth, then washed it down with delicate sips of his tea.

"Well," Bates resumed, slapping his knees in a gesture of finality, "we've got to be on our way."

As he and Urban began to rise, Takashi tinkled the small silver bell at his side. He also reached behind his back, under a supporting pillow, and brought forth two sets of papers, each the size of a big city telephone directory.

Simultaneously, tape-recorded sounds began emanating from surround-around speakers cleverly hidden in the garden.

Bates and Urban were stopped in their tracks, their mouths stunned open. Theirs and Takashi's voices were clearly discernible, discussing in an obviously condensed and edited format, a wide and incredibly incriminating series of operations.

"Velly, solly, genemens," Takashi purred with honed sarcasm, "but that's only a tiny sampling. I or my environment was wired for practically every, shall we say, critical engagement, ever since I arrived. Those," pointing to the thick paper books, "comprise a fraction of the transcriptions. However, they alone are more than enough to cause great agitation."

When it appeared the two agents were about to explode, Takashi raised a skeletal hand and continued,

"When you've had time to reflect, you'll appreciate how carefully I prepared for this eventuality. I am anything but a fool. All my evidence, boxes and boxes, have been duplicated, vacuum sealed, and sent very secretly to various parts of the world. The recipients are as unaware of the contents as you are of the recipients. Their only instructions are to the effect that if I should disappear or fail to transmit a periodic coded signal, or if I should die, they will immediately let the cats out of the bags. It is fail safe. I know it. You know it. You haven't a clue as to how the tracks can be retraced. And you have time to make a judicious career shift. Deal?"

"You may have us by the cajones, little man," Bates replied through gritting teeth, "but you'd also be throwing your own scrawny hide into the frying pan."

"Ah, yes," Takashi said, stroking the slim scraggle of white beard on his wrinkled chin, "but I am very old and you are still relatively young. Besides, as your FDR said, the only thing you have to fear is fear itself. So long as I am left alone to do as I please, your secrets are secure. But try recovering one of the damning sets, and it's pop goes the weasel. Deal?"

Bates looked at Urban, shrugged his shoulders, and mumbled, "Deal."

# SEVEN

Three strapping young men waited contentedly as Amy McNeill and Mimi Revere snipped the hair of two of their buddies outside the girls' little log cabin. It was situated about fifteen miles from Kalispell in northwest Montana, three strides from a fast-flowing stream from which Amy and Mimi extracted beautiful rainbow trout, equipped only with broom handles, string, and whatever fly was appropriate for the day.

It was a monthly ritual. The men, all in their early twenties and college graduates except for one, came in one pick-up. In exchange for the shearing, they'd do a variety of odd jobs. One included tinkering with Amy's and Mimi's rusted Volkswagen van. Amy had pleaded with her father for the loan to purchase the relic because it was needed to get to work at LibertyAire Chemical and to transport the equipment the girls used to manicure the burgeoning number of lawns being acquired by the tourons, the epithet applied to wealthy doctors, lawyers, and businessmen who streamed in mostly from the detested California. Landscaping was a way for them to earn additional income, surreptitiously tax free.

For Amy, the clincher for acquisition was the fact the van was owned by a preacher. To her father, Colonel John McNeill, it was a reason to seal your purse and run. He relented, however, and Amy and Mimi quickly lived to rue the day. They'd acquired a lemon the size of a cantaloupe.

Nonetheless, their freebie hair-cut customers kept the beast moving.

They'd do much more, almost anything, to have an excuse to be in the company of their barbers. Amy was five-two, curly-honey blond, with devastating blue eyes, an exquisite figure, and a generous, perfect smile emanating from a flawless, sun-bronzed face.

Mimi had the same height, proportions, and smile, but her soft straight hair was radiantly auburn, her eyes as green as emeralds.

In short, the fellows agreed, they were to die for.

As she snipped away at Jerry Duncan's locks, Mimi declared emphatically, "If you go ahead with this cockamamie stunt of Amy's and anything goes wrong, I'll hold you responsible. You hear?"

Jerry Duncan, a ruggedly handsome, dark-complexioned six footer, shrugged under the apron tied around his neck that served as a makeshift barber cloth.

"You've got dangerous weapons in your hands, Mimi," Jerry said. "What can I say, other than you're beautiful when you're mad. Besides, Amy says a deal's a deal. She's right, you know."

"Men," Mimi hissed.

"Oh, Mimi, come down from the pulpit," Amy joshed, as she cut the hair of the gargantuan blond, Swede Olsen, "you're making a mountain out of a molehill. Isn't that so, Swede?"

Swede Olsen could clean out any bar in Montana, single handed. But when it came to confronting or contradicting a female, he was all putty.

"Aw, c'mon, Amy, gimme a break," he pleaded, letting it drop there.

"What's your beef, Mimi?" Crazy Louie Morgan asked, as he sat on an empty barrel. The Crazy part of his name was never mentioned in his company, but it was recognized by all, nonetheless. He was not much taller than the girls, maybe five-four, with a cadaverous face, pinched cheeks, and very deepset eyes, the only one among them who hadn't gone to college. It was common knowledge that he adored Amy. Not in a romantic sense. She'd simply been the kindest, sweetest, most caring, and nonjudgmental person he'd ever encountered.

On countless occasions Amy had driven to Crazy's forest teepee in the dead of a bitter winter, tapped him awake from a frozen slumber, helped him get to her van to thaw out, then gave him some warm nourishment.

Louie had gotten the moniker Crazy from his caveman uncontrollability of booze. Normally docile and courteous, he'd go bananas with a few shots under his belt, incredibly more than a match for the first few men to take him on. The sheriff had spread the word that nobody, under any circumstance, was to serve him any form of liquor, or suffer the consequences. If it came to it, Crazy Louie would probably kill for Amy.

"What's my beef?" Mimi asked Crazy Louie with an uncharacteristic sting in her voice. "I'll tell you my beef. Your stupid friend Jerry here is going to chopper Amy fifty miles out to the boonies next weekend, plunk her down, and leave her on her silly own to make her way back all by herself.

"She could twist an ankle, get nailed by a rattler, or chased down and eaten by a grizzly, or black bear, or cougar. She's having her period. You've all heard the stories about how grizzlies get off on that scent. It's like ringing a dinner bell right under their chins. As for all her vaunted abilities, Amy cannot, repeat cannot, outrun a bear or mountain lion."

Crazy Louie looked adoringly at Amy and smiled, humming the old Ray Bolger hit, "Once in Love with Amy."

Amy said soothingly, "I'll be just fine. I'll have chow to last me more than three days, a good, lightweight snuggie, a map and compass. A breeze. It's not the first time I've hiked solo, y'know."

The men, excepting the noncommital Swede, nodded in agreement.

"Sure, take her side," Mimi bristled. "How about the times she got treed by bears while out there communing with nature and plucking wildflowers?"

"Oh, Mimi," Amy sighed impatiently. "Black bears hardly ever chase people, even though they can climb. Grizzlies can't climb."

"No, but a grizzly can sure as hell knock down a good-size Indian lodge pole or pine," Mimi retorted, "and those big cats can climb like squirrels. And what about rattlers? They're shedding their skins now and don't even make a sound before they strike."

Jeff Curry, another six-footer who was as dark as Swede was light, took Jerry's place as the next barber customer and saw an opportunity to lighten or at least divert the conversation.

Addressing Crazy Louie, he asked, "You working on that new home they're building near Lake Magnifique?"

"Yep, been at it more'n a month now," Crazy said. "Gonna be a doozie. Neighborhood of two, three million smackeroos. Pay's great. Met the owner. Nice guy. Speaks good American. Real old. Looks like a chink."

"I think he's the same old bird I saw being shown around LibertyAire," Mike Smith chimed in. Mike had a carrot top, light blue eyes, and the freckles to match. "Hear they brought him in from somewhere out east," he continued. "Supposed to be a hotshot consultant for that new contract on disposal of toxic chemicals."

"He'd better be good." Amy frowned as she motioned Mike to take Swede's place for a shearing. "They're going to be hauling that junk in by the ton; hundreds of different chemicals. It's why Mimi and I got our jobs with LibertyAire. Two kids fresh out of high school and we're supposed to help monitor how all that stuff is disposed of on public lands. We can check the soil for contaminants, but it's really somebody like my dad who should be supervising, not some codger who's probably been brought in for window dressing and can't walk more than twenty feet at a stretch."

When they'd finished the hair cutting, Mimi asked, "Anyone for a Coke?" She'd caught herself just in time. She had been about to say beer until she realized Crazy Louie was among the invitees.

Mike Smith went quickly behind the cabin and pulled on the rope that descended into the deep, cold stream, extracting a basket containing a dozen Coke cans.

"While you're here," Amy said, "one of you guys check the leak in our shower, okay?"

Jerry Duncan followed Amy inside the cabin, looked at the source of the dripping, and said, "Piece of cake, darlin'. Gotta get a couple tools from the truck. Back in a jiff."

When the young men left, Mimi surveyed the two-room cabin. It wasn't much but they'd made the most of it. Cheap rent for cheap accommodations. A splintery table with two rickety chairs, a pot-bellied stove, a dinky bathroom with an irregular shower, a foot-pumped sewing machine from which they'd fashioned much of their clothing, and chintz curtains, a U of M pennant on a wall, a spin top-looking implement with which they replaced the soles of their boondocks, and no telephone. Calls were taken and placed from a neighborhood saloon, The Skull Popper.

The girls were soul mates from college, establishing Montana residency for a year to qualify for lower tuition. In a tight economy, they were thrilled to land jobs with LibertyAire Chemical, although both felt pangs of guilt over an employer that typified much of what was going amiss in the environment.

Amy came inside and flashed a mischievous grin.

Mimi caught it and said, "I think you're up to something with this hiking escapade that you haven't told me about. Right?"

"I don't keep secrets from my bunkie. Let's go grab a pizza."

# EIGHT

As Colonel John McNeill looked out from center stage at the attendees for his wind-up lecture, he noticed a significant change in its pedigree. There were dozens of newcomers displaying the ranks of generals and admirals, as well as expensively tailored civilians. There were dramatic military and industrial changes to be faced in the near future, and the audience wanted to hear the distinguished speaker's appraisal of them.

"Ladies and gentlemen, my name's John McNeill. We've discussed in considerable detail the implications of chemical and biological weaponry. I trust I won't sound glib or naive when I say that it would not be very productive to harp further on the biological phase of our review. Granted, such weapons are horrifying almost beyond description. That's my point. Once released in whatever form, but especially those that have been genetically engineered, they are uncontrollable, virtually suicidal. Open the bottle that spews viruses, bacteria, rickettsiae, and or a litany of natural toxins, the monster could turn on its master. In this era of heavy intercontinental travel, to say nothing of wind gusts, you can't fence in blind killers like plague, cholera, ebola, typhoid, and dozens more of their ilk. It's ironic, like owning a rifle with a history of firing simultaneously to the front and rear. Only a self-destructing lunatic would give it a second thought.

"Chemical warfare is a different breed of cat. It can be relatively cheap and easy to manufacture in secrecy at small facilities which, among other liabilities, are susceptible to terrorist theft. Such plants can also be made to appear completely innocent within hours, notably those that are ostensibly in the business of pesticides and drugs.

"In binary arrangements whereby toxic chemicals mix while fired from cannons or dropped in bombs, they are safe to store and transport. Another maddening aspect lies in the ability of concocting a brew of two separate and harmless ingredients into something quite deadly. But the most critical factor in the chemical warfare scenario is, within limits, being able to confine the impact, making chemicals a more tempting alternative.

"So where does that leave us? In my opinion, we're in a mixed bag. More than a lick and a promise, but still a long way from being safe at home plate. At the start of this decade, Congress failed to put a lid on companies and governments that dealt in chemical or biological weapons.

"Fortunately, that setback was temporary. Earlier this year the International Chemical Weapons Convention was born. The United States anticipated the signatories by having already started the destruction of stored chemical arms in scads of shelters, with a completion targeted for the end of the century. The former Soviet bloc is looking toward two thousand two, at a price that will run into the tens of billions. That's a lot for an economic basket case.

"In short, there's cause for restrained celebration. Worries remain. The chemical treaty involves two possible time lags. It'll take effect two years from the day it was open for membership among the nations, or six months after sixty-five nations sign and ratify. The time is needed to set up worldwide inspections. To the cynical, myself included, it also presents opportunities for stockpiling and related subterfuges.

"Sadly, our world is less than ideal. Blunt questions persist. How many hold-outs will there be to the convention? My answer, too many. We all know how Iraq, for one glaring example, has lied through its teeth, damning evidence notwithstanding. Recall also that it was only last year that Boris Yeltsin acknowledged that the nineteen seventy-nine epidemic of anthrax at Yakaterinburg, the former Sverdlovsk, was not due to meat contamination but to an alleged accident at a germ warfare plant.

"The point, ladies and gentlemen, is that there has been ample room to lie, stonewall, and cover up without genuine fear of reprisal, either militarily, politically, or economically.

"Here's another dilly. Will mandatory advance notices on verification inspections effectively preclude discovery of violators? I'm afraid so. How many shell-game operators fold their tables and disappear when a look-out spots a cop? That analogy is close to the mark. Pint-size chemical operations can be made to change appearances as fast as a chameleon.

"Bear with me. We're nearing the wind-up. Will stiff sanctions finally be imposed against violators? Look at the record. You tell me who's ever been really nailed for chemical warfare. No, let me tell you. Nobody. It's previously always come down to the political question of whose ox is being gored, enemy or foe? A mutt that won't bite is no watchdog.

"Finally, some of you asked me prior to this little session what I felt the reaction would be among those who are asked to scuttle all facets of chemical arms while we and the Russians have an extended time-frame to clean out our own stables. I think they're likely to take the position of the child who's warned by a pot-smoking parent not to try marijuana."

"I don't get it," Amy said as Mimi wheeled their venerable van through the guarded, chain-link fence entrance to LibertyAire Chemical Company. They displayed their picture I.D.'s.

"Don't get what?"

"I figured we'd be seeing caravans of semis lined up here with toxic chemicals we're supposed to be getting rid of. Instead, all we've seen are more of the same ones that've been coming all along, hauling that stuff they use to make ink for ballpoint pens and put into textiles. What's it called again?"

"Thiodiglycol," Mimi answered.

"Yeh, right, have to remember that," Amy said. "So maybe all that scuttlebutt about getting a big government contract to dispose of chemical weapons is a lot of malarkey. If that's the case, why do they need us to take samples of the vegetation for a mile around?"

Mimi drove to their assigned parking place, stopped, and looked around. The LibertyAire building was impressive from almost any perspective. It was two rectangular stories of white brick, three hundred yards by two hundred. There were no windows on the lower, manufacturing and storage level and heavily amber-tinted ones on the second, where the offices and laboratories operated. Its velvety lawn was festooned with colorful domestic stone surrounding a wide variety of trees, bushes, and flowers.

"I think we're hired hands to help placate the locals who don't work here," Mimi said. "Just about everybody gets a little nervous when they're near a big chemical operation, and this sucker is big. If they can show the clean-air people, the government, and the news media that they're really into monitoring for the public's safety, the cost is peanuts and they've preempted a big p.r. promotion.

"Besides," Mimi continued, "Jerry and Jeff have been put on a beefed-up night shift. They say there's a lot of trucks been coming here after dark. Funny thing, though."

"Funny what?" Amy asked.

"They say all those barrels that come in one night are shipped out the next. Sounds goofy to me."

"What're they hauling?" Amy persisted.

"I haven't a clue. Neither do the guys. No labels on the barrels. I'm sure they'll tell us when they're ready. Let's get inside or we'll miss the punch-in time. By the way, have you noticed there are a lot more guards around here lately? Jeff and Jerry said they started patroling with dobermans at night, too."

Jerry Duncan waved delightedly as the familiar, de-crepit Volkswagen van chugged toward the small but sleek helicopter he was warming up.

"If your old man wasn't such a filthy rich rancher, you wouldn't be doing this silly stunt," Mimi shouted through the van window as she pulled just beyond reach of the copter's slow-moving rotor blade.

"Morning, Jerry," Amy greeted. "As you can tell, Mimi had a whole box of conviviality pills for breakfast."

"Love her anyway," Jerry responded. "This it?" he asked as he hefted Amy's backpack and placed it in the helicopter's cabin.

"It's all I need," Amy answered.

"You be careful now, you little nitwit," Mimi said, embracing her best friend.

"Don't be a worry wart," Amy said, exchanging the hug. "I'll be back, safe and sound, before you know it."

The next moment the copter was airborne, moving confidently at an altitude of five hundred feet, an ideal height to enjoy northwest Montana's stunning beauty.

After they'd cruised leisurely for about twenty-five minutes, Amy checked the compass and peered down from an elevation of several hundred feet. Sure enough, at roughly two hundred seventy degrees, she spotted the same road she'd seen under construction on a similar journey last spring. Only this time the two-lane route was obviously completed. Weird. It emerged from mountainous forest, continued for a quarter mile or so across a narrow valley, then ducked into more forest. Her pilot didn't seem to notice the oddity.

When they'd flown a few more miles, Amy signaled Jerry to descend. He picked a spot and eased the helicopter down to a convenient spot flanked by mountains and trees. It was still only late afternoon.

Jerry helped Amy adjust her backpack, kissed her softly, and said, "Good luck, beautiful."

"Thanks, driver. See you back at the ranch. Look in on Mimi."

Jerry took off, waving.

Mimi took out her compass, sighted in on a distinctive mountain peak that aligned with the ninety-degree heading she wanted, then began jogging toward her first objective.

She wore porous but sturdy hiking boots, knee-high double-soled sox, and matching green shorts, shirt, and cap.

She was happy and excited. She knew she had hours to get to the mysterious road and see if she could finally satisfy her curiosity. She knew it wouldn't be really dark until roughly ten o'clock. Even then, on such a clear evening, the moon and stars would be like big natural candles helping a careful traveler keep going if need be.

She stopped to pick up and enjoy a few Indian paintbrush flowers and stuck them in the cord that lined her cap.

While stopped, she took a long moment to survey the surroundings. She discovered she was pretty much in open, grassy field, close by a stream on her right and perhaps a hundred yards from a stand of lodge pole trees that worked up a mountainside to her left.

Because the distance was so short, Amy decided to go to the stream, splash some water on her warm face and arms, then work her way up the timberline as a safety precaution.

As she worked her way through bullrushes to the quick flowing steam, she suddenly saw paw prints as big as dinner plates.

"Grizzly," she whispered. Only one North American beast made that kind of mark, and it had to be a real jumbo. Worse, the imprint was wet, indicating the owner had visited the place very recently.

Amy thumbed the straps on her back and moved toward the forest as fast as she could in a crouch. After she'd traveled some thirty yards hunched over, she straightened up and broke into an all-out run.

As she approached the skinny lodge poles, she looked back and cried, "God!"

Coming at her at full speed was a mass that looked like a hairy locomotive, breathing clearly audible grunts that signaled unbridled fury.

Amy dropped her pack and scrambled, panic stricken, past the feeble trees, searching desperately for anything climbable or that would offer some kind of defense.

She turned to see that the bear had stopped to examine the discarded pack. In seconds, its treacherous mouth had ripped it to shreds. Angrily, it cuffed aside the few pieces of clothing and canned goods, found some slices of elk jerky and gobbled them down, plastic wrapping and all.

It looked toward where Amy had headed and resumed its outraged quest.

In seconds, Amy's prayer for reprieve was dashed by the sight of the hard-charging bear and the realization its brief distraction had failed to reveal a tree big enough to climb and strong enough to withstand a ton of thunderous onslaught.

With the realization she had nothing to lose except her life, she ran toward where some thick logs had been felled. They'd fallen rather tightly together over what she sensed could be a cave or a hole.

The bear was within ten years when Amy wiggled through a miraculous two-foot opening. Just big enough for her. God willing, not big enough for the grizzly, but heavy enough to be immovable.

The bear raged at the obstruction, protruding as much of its monstrous head inside the slit as possible, baring long, yellow fangs, and rolling its small, bloodshot eyes.

Amy looked frantically about. There was still ample light to discover the obvious. There was no other way out. She was trapped in a hole no more than twenty feet long, without food or water, and the devil was at her door.

The bear clawed violently at the log barrier, smashing it so hard it seemed as though its parts would submit at any moment.

In spite of being frightened to tears, Amy approached the logs to tear away some slim bark strips. Her movements only served to reinvigorate the bear's assault.

As she amassed a solid handful of bark, she felt in her shirt pocket and pulled out a pack of matches. She lit the bundle and, when the attacker next stuck its gnashing snout between the slits, she rammed the torch into its face.

The grizzly screamed but backed away, licking its nose and smelling the burnt flesh.

Amy kept moving the torch across the logs, starting a series of little fires, which quickly converged to form a spreading blaze.

The grizzly took a couple of frustrated slaps at the budding fire but gave up. It could conquer almost anything on earth but fire. It lumbered off, heading back for the stream where it had probably been hunting for trout.

Amy watched the retreat in disbelief. When she felt confident the bear had resigned itself to failure, she threw handfuls of dirt on the fire, extinguishing it in ten minutes. She knew she'd have to wait until heat had expired sufficiently to enable her to crawl back out. She was in no hurry, anyway. She resigned herself to spending the night right where she was.

After her terror subsided, however, Amy had an abrupt change of heart. She looked around anxiously, peering to the depth of the emergency dwelling. She could discern moist rock at the farthest point, shimmering in the light admitted through the log cracks.

She felt her arms. They were cool. The shelter was cool. It was an ideal setting for rattlers. She recalled Mimi's admonition, that it was their skin-peeling season and that they did not rattle before striking. Too, she wondered whether Mimi was prescient in warning about the effect women going through their monthly curse had on stinking bears that had radar in their noses.

Hurriedly, Amy began pitching more dirt on the logs as she looked to the rear every few seconds. She peeped through the opening, saw no sign of the bear, and decided to risk being singed by the logs rather than bitten with venomous fangs.

She crawled through. If there was heat from the logs, her anxious mind refused to acknowledge it.

There was still plenty of visibility. Cautiously, ready in a second to dive back into the shelter with its alternate and frightening potential, she scampered to where the grizzly had discovered her backpack. It was in tatters, as were her change of underwear and light sleeping bag.

Glancing furtively back and forth from the ground to the stream and its camouflaging bull rushes, she saw several cans of food and retrieved them.

Widening her search she soon discovered her can opener, compass, a torn but still usable map, small binoculars, remarkably intact, and a packet containing three sanitary napkins. She strung the binoculars around her neck and stuffed all but the compass and map into her pants, grateful that she had decided to wear shorts with deep, bulky pockets instead of sexy hip huggers. The one item she regretted not finding was her canteen.

Ever on the alert, she sighted through the compass on two prominent locations, read the bearings, and reversed the degree readings, drawing lines with her ballpoint pen on the map.

Now that she'd determined her approximate location she pocketed the compass and map and moved up the mountainside in a generally easterly direction, heading toward the mystery road.

Amy was soon pleased to confirm the guess that trees would be sturdier and more abundant as she climbed. Along with providing handier and more reliable recourse in the event of another bear encounter, the higher elevation would permit a much wider survey point.

Because she was young and in excellent physical condition, Amy moved at a quick pace. There were plenty of trees, but they were not crammed together, allowing better all-around visibility with which she could check her bearings. Another advantage was that the rocky ground was almost free of grasses and prickly bushes, minimizing somewhat the element of a surprise attack from rattlers that favored tall, dry grass.

Her wristwatch indicated the military time of eighteen fifty, or six-thirty P.M. Again referring to her map and compass, she calculated she should be looking down on the road approximately fifteen hundred feet below in less than half an hour.

The half-hour passed and she kept looking and hiking. She saw no road and was puzzled. She thought she saw the right valley, bordered by thick forest. Where the road should have been, there was nothing but a solid covering of deep green grass.

Amy came across a narrow stream and suddenly realized how terribly thirsty she was. She looked up to the peak of the mountain, at least six thousand feet high and snow-capped. She'd long since learned that drinking from streams, no matter the origin or how pristine looking, carried the risk of swallowing water that contained animal excrement. She opted for the drink, anyway.

She looked around, more out of modesty than apprehension, pushed down her shorts and panties, changed the Kotex, rinsed herself, and re-clothed. She worked a stubby branch into the rugged ground, digging down about six inches, buried the soiled napkin under dirt and stones, and washed her hands with water and sand.

As she was rechecking her map and compass, wondering whether the latter was defective, Amy was startled by a muted rumbling sound from below.

Open-mouthed, she watched in fascination as the valley's green grass parted, revealing the quarter-mile road. At the same time, the eastern portion of the forest raised as though it were on an escalator, to a height of about twenty feet.

Amy sprinted along and down the mountainside and adjusted her binoculars.

She was startled again. From within the forest whose "door" had been raised some twenty feet, she could make out a mid-size tractor. It was pulling an airplane to the entrance, an executive-type twin-engined jet!

Scrambling farther down, ducking behind trees and rocks, Amy could see that whatever was behind the opening extended to an indeterminable depth.

The tractor driver unhitched the plane, made two signals, and drove back inside.

Immediately, a large camouflaged, chimneylike pipe protruded straight up about fifteen feet close to the entrance. The jet's engines roared as the plane moved forward. A flap atop the chimney fluttered.

Amy realized the road was in actuality a small runway and that the chimney was the capper on a ventilation system. Admittedly ignorant about aircraft, she still couldn't imagine how anything aside from a helicopter or special military combat plane could take off in such a short distance. Or land. Which raised the question as to whether the forest on the opposite side of the runway opened and closed, also.

One question was settled momentarily. The silvery jet screamed down the runway and ascended vertically like a rocket, with room to spare.

In seconds, the chimney dropped, the opening closed, and the runway was covered with artificial grass.

Amy sat in disbelief, a hundred questions running through her head.

Her ruminating was abruptly interrupted by the loud cracking sound of a sizable branch breaking. She turned to see, perhaps forty yards away, a huge grizzly galloping toward her. It was, unquestionably, the same monster that had stalked her earlier.

Amy screamed and began climbing a lodge pole tree that had a presumably immovable circumference yet one that she could negotiate.

She screamed again at the realization the bear had erased the distance between them so quickly that one of its claws would have snared a boot if she had wasted a fraction of a second in her ascent.

The bear raged, clawed, and even bit the tree as Amy kept climbing to a branch big enough to support her, screaming as she climbed.

The grizzly circled the tree, alternately on all fours and hind legs.

Amy found the limb she was searching for and straddled it, her arms embracing the tree. She continued screaming as the bear continued to roar. It seemed to announce that it wasn't about to abandon its quest this time.

Amy felt temporarily safe, but she knew she would not have the strength to simply hold on interminably. She resumed her screaming.

Looking down, her cap falling off, she saw the bear shudder repeatedly, then heard the report of powerful automatic gunfire. The grizzly was covered in blood as it slumped soundlessly to the ground.

Two rough-looking men dressed in camouflage outfits came up to Amy's tree and poked at the bear with their rifle muzzles.

One looked up and said, "Come on down, Goldilocks. Your friend ain't gonna play with you no more."

Amy climbed down and said, "Thanks, fellas, you saved my life. Now, can you get me to a phone so I can arrange to be picked up?"

The one who had invited her to climb down grinned through hard, dark eyes and replied, "Sorry, cupcake, but our boss'll want to talk to you. So you just figure on being our guest for a while."

# NINE

Master Sergeant Oscar Riley sat in his office outside that of Colonel John McNeill's at the marine base in Quantico, Virginia, filling out his retirement papers. He'd come early this Wednesday morning to preclude impinging on his regular work routine.

The process prodded memories full of many twists and curves and that began in that long-ago year of nineteen sixty-eight in Vietnam, when he served under then Second Lieutenant McNeill.

On balance, he decided it had been a career much more of pluses than minuses. True, he could've made it to sergeant major, with all the heady powers that senior noncommissioned rank entailed. He'd had all the credentials, including an imposing command presence, years dotted with steady promotions and sterling fitness reports, and the sort of service real marines were supposed to experience in Vietnam, in Grenada, and, again with Colonel McNeill, in Desert Storm.

He was not only delighted but proud to have been selected as Colonel McNeill's top NCO. Delighted because he admired his boss as a brave and brilliant professional who cared deeply about his subordinates, in peace and war. Proud because he was an African-American who'd made it to the NCO's pinnacle, and had done it on his own merits.

He stood and walked to the small adjoining laboratory, where his colonel would spend hours at a time, poring over cultures and microscopes. Hands on hips, he searched the room for anything short of spotlessness. He had the hard glare and appearance of a drill sergeant examining the rifle of a raw recruit. His shoes gleamed, his khaki uniform looked as though it could mow a lawn, and the brass buckle on the belt that surrounded his trim waist shone like gold.

Satisfied everything in the lab was in perfect order, he looked inside the colonel's room. Every book and reference had been replaced, the desk was highly polished, the chairs and windows freshly dusted.

He smiled and whispered, "Beautiful," as he glanced at the desk's triple eight-by-ten photos of Julie and Amy McNeill, and Mimi Revere.

He returned to his desk and resumed looking at his service record. Recollections of Vietnam flooded back, of Corporal Tommy Napoli, Noobie Girard, Boomer Wiley, Agent Orange, and a flight that looked like it meant he and all the others had surely bought the farm.

"Gotta drop Tommy and Boomer a card," he said, scribbling a note to that effect. They'd stayed in touch over the years, especially Napoli, who was constantly inviting him to come to Las Vegas, on the house.

"Good morning, Top," John McNeill said cheerfully as he opened the door.

"Good morning, sir," an immediately bolt upright Oscar Riley responded.

"Anything hot?" McNeill asked.

"Nothing pressing, sir. Looks like we're both in final countdown for the last hurrah. Let's hope it stays this way," Riley answered with a huge smile.

"Roger that," McNeill said as he opened his office door, characteristically leaving it wide ajar. He started shuffling through a pile of mail and other correspondence centered on his desk.

A telephone rang. "Colonel McNeill's office, Master Sergeant Riley, sir." When one served as aide to a senior officer, it was assumed any caller was an officer, likely a very senior one.

"One moment, please, miss," Riley said as he pressed the intercom.

"What've you got, Top?" the colonel responded.

"Miss Mimi Revere calling from Montana, sir."

McNeill frowned, glancing at his watch, noting it would be five o'clock in the morning Montana time.

"How's my Little Red Riding Hood?" he inquired, shifting his eyes to Mimi's photo.

"I'm fine, John, thank you. And you?"

McNeill loved Mimi's informality. "Couldn't be better. What's up, sweetheart?"

"Amy's missing. She took one of her solo hikes in the boonies last Friday afternoon. A friend took her by helicopter to somewhere near Jezebel Pass. We expected her back no later than Sunday."

McNeill gripped the phone hard. "Have the authorities been notified?"

"State police, sheriff's office, and the forest rangers. Jerry Duncan, the guy who flew her out, has been up scouring the place for hours. He's on a real guilt trip. He's had a crush on Amy ever since he laid eyes on her. 'Course, what guy wouldn't?"

"I'm on my way, Mimi. Where you calling from?"

"The Skull Popper."

"Give me the number."

Mimi complied.

"I'll call in transit. If you're there, fine. If not, I'll leave a message. If you have any word to pass, you do the same."

"Check, John, and Godspeed. But you know it won't be fast or easy getting a commercial flight here. Montana's still pretty much a whistle stop for the airlines."

McNeill knew she was right but said, "Don't worry, hon. I'll be there in quick time."

As soon as they hung up, McNeill said to Master Sergeant Riley, "Get General DeGrazia at Cherry Point on the horn."

"Yes, sir."

When the call was placed, Riley signaled McNeill, who picked up his phone.

"General DeGrazia's headquarters, Captain Luca, sir."

"Captain, please inform the general that Colonel John McNeill would like to speak with him."

"John!" DeGrazia's voice exploded through the receiver. "How the hell are you?"

"Could be better, General."

"Hold it. Anybody who risks his life to save my dago buns, my name is Pug, even if I become commandant."

McNeill smiled, despite his concern. "Thanks, Pug. I just got word my daughter Amy's missing somewhere in the wilds of Montana, near Kalispel. Sounds serious."

"I'm sorry as hell to hear that. What can I do?"

"Can you swing me a fighter hop?"

"For you, I can do better than that. How soon can you shove off?"

"I'll tell my C.O. to have Top expedite the cutting of orders, and toss some stuff in a suitcase. I can be standing by ready to go in a half hour."

"Good," DeGrazia exclaimed. "Get to your field. I'll have a chopper zip you down here. I'll have a fighter jet waiting for a flight to Pendleton by way of Kalispel. The plane can park on a postage stamp. You'll be there in time for a Montoony breakfast."

"Thanks, Pug."

"Forget it. I still owe you."

# TEN

Major General Pug DeGrazia had been good as his word. It was still morning in Montana when the marine fighter jet bearing John McNeill eased down at Kalispell as softly as a feather, seemingly requiring only as much room as the postage stamp Pug had alluded to.

"Thanks a million, Lieutenant," McNeill said to the handsome young pilot. "That was some ride. Glad to know you're on our side."

"You're welcome, sir, and thank *you*. You're my ticket to California, a layover at Pendleton, and a chance to see some sights and grab a meal that isn't dished up in a BOQ."

The two shook hands. McNeill grabbed his bag and got down from the plane, immediately after which it taxied for takeoff.

McNeill went inside the small airport, signed up for a Ford car rental, and got courteous answers to several questions he posed to an obviously impressed attendant. It wasn't every day a passenger appeared out of a marine jet fighter.

The colonel, in civvies, was pleased a car was readily available. He drove it onto U.S. 93 for a few miles until he saw a sign on a wooden upside-down L post reading, in burned-on lettering, "The Skull Popper Saloon."

Despite the still-morning hours, the parking lot was packed, presumably the early lunch bunch, including those on liquid diets.

Most of the thirty or so vehicles on the wooden-fenced, dirt lot were weatherbeaten pickups, each invariably containing a hunting rifle racked across and inside the rear window.

In addition, there were several motorcycles, heavy-duty Harleys gussied up with sparklers as well as two-foot-long animal tails streaming from the handlebar grips.

Next door was an unappealing motel. McNeill drove on a mile or so until he saw one that suggested at least a modicum of sanitation. It billed itself as "The White Grizzly." He went into the office, which was half the size of a small bedroom. The clerk, probably part of a mom-and-pop ownership, was a thirtyish dishwater blond, with too much weight and makeup. But, she offered a friendly smile, looked like she bathed regularly, and the office was clean.

He signed up, tenatively, for overnight, retaining the option of extending if it seemed appropriate.

McNeill went to his room, number eight, one of twelve on line in a single-story log structure flanked by gravel and empty flower pots.

Inside was one narrow bed, a pillow and an Indian blanket, a small table with a lamp and sixty-watt bulb, a two-drawer dresser with a nineteen-inch TV that promised no more than a single channel, and a bathroom with a heavily chipped sink, a discolored and cracked mirror, a matchbox shower, half a roll of toilet paper atop a weather-stained toilet, and clean but almost transparent washcloth and towel. No soap.

McNeill shrugged. At least he had yet to see a cockroach.

He opened his heavy suitcase, pulled out a field camouflage outfit and boots, and exchanged them for his gray slacks, red sport shirt, and loafers. He locked up and drove his economy four-door back to The Skull Popper.

As he was taking the one step up to the saloon's duck-board porch, a tall, husky, moon-faced Indian, dressed in fawn-colored leather and moccasins, came out through the swinging doors.

He looked at McNeill through large brown eyes and asked, "You go in there?" pointing at the swinging doors.

Surprised, McNeill smiled and nodded. "You a Blackfoot?"

The Indian nodded, adding, "Bad men in there."

McNeill said, "Thanks," and passed through the doors.

McNeill knew he'd look out of place. But after a few curious stares, his novelty quickly dissipated.

The sight, odors, and sounds were fairly predictable. Tobacco smoke filled the air. Loud recorded Western music induced louder conversation and laughter. All but a very few of the clientele wore ten-gallon hats, blue jeans with large metal buckles, and ornamental, varicolored cowboy shirts and high-heel leather boots. The walls were lined with antlers of various origins and sizes.

Two-thirds of the crowd were lined along a mahagony bar, a brass rail, sawdust, and spittoons at their feet. The rest were scattered among venerable chairs at seven sturdy, claw-foot tables.

Two dyed brunette barmaids in tight T-shirts, ciga-rettes dangling from their thick reddened lips, hustled to keep up with the demands for beer and house whiskey. In a corner, another, older woman worked energetically be-hind a half-walled counter on a large roast, fashioning piles of sandwiches lathered with horseradish. Roast beef seemed to be the only food being offered. A shy teenage boy made the rounds, scribbling food orders.

At the opposite corner, seated by himself, McNeill saw one of the biggest men he'd ever encountered, a truly im-mense Indian, probably a Blackfoot like the one who warned him at the door. Behind him was the public telephone.

This Indian, too, was dressed in Indian regalia. But he had a mean, angry face, his black eyes boring into the back of a heavy, thick armed and bearded biker at the bar. The object of his attention was dressed in black leather from head to foot, his hairy torso covered only by a rhinestone vest. From under his cap grew a three-foot long, braided pony tail. On either side of him were two other drinking motorcycle companions, similarly dressed, but whose unkempt hair was only shoulder length.

McNeill took a chair near the doorway, deciding it would be better to wait until the hubbub died down somewhat before he inquired whether Mimi may've left a message for him. If not, he'd get the number and call her at LibertyAire.

No sooner had he sat down than a short, scrawny newcomer entered alone.

"Well, dear me, if it ain't Crazy Louie," a gap-toothed barfly yelled. A crony laughed and added, "Come in for a little catnip, Crazy?"

"Up yours," the newcomer bristled.

McNeill got up and tapped him on the shoulder. Crazy whirled around with clenched fists and fire in his eyes. "What the hell do you want?" he demanded.

McNeill smiled and held out placating hands. "Easy, fella. My name's John McNeill. I believe you're a friend of my daughter Amy."

Crazy Louie Morgan's face lit up. Extending his right hand, he said, "I'm sure as tootin' Amy's friend, and I'm right proud to shake your hand."

"Will you join me for a little while?" McNeill asked.

Crazy nodded, the smile gone, and sat down.

61

The saloon went suddenly almost quiet. At first, McNeill thought it was due to his invitation to Crazy. Then he noticed most of the patrons were looking at the jumbo Indian walking from his corner table toward the bar. The waitresses rolled their eyes and moved toward the open kitchen. Others among the veteran clientele at the bar smirked, nudged, and moved nonchalantly away from the bikers, none of whom seemed aware that something unusual was afoot.

"Trouble comin'," Crazy Louie said to McNeill.

The big Indian grabbed the middle biker's thick ponytail, pulled back violently, then smashed his face on the bar surface. As he repeated the violent move, the attacker whipped out a long hunting knife and cut off the ponytail, casting it aside as though it were a detestable snake.

The other bikers, too stunned to react, soon felt their faces being smashed together, several times in quick succession. With masks of blood, they fell in a heap beside their de-ponytailed companion.

The big Indian sheathed his knife and, one by one, hurled the bikes through the swinging doors.

While the kid waiter came with broom and dust pan to sweep away the bloodied sawdust, a wag at the bar said, "Old chief don't like competition when it comes to hair. Betcha them guys won't be poppin' into The Skull Popper for quite a spell."

The remark brought a burst of laughter, which ended quickly.

The Indian glared around the room, then turned to fix his stare on McNeill and Crazy Louie, who were seated three feet away.

Looking at McNeill while pointing at Crazy, he said, "No booze for him."

"And no more sneak attacks by you, eh, Wahoo?" McNeill replied evenly, his gray eyes narrowing.

The crowd was stunned. Crazy looked at McNeill as though he were a man who'd blithely put his head under the blade of a guillotine.

When, after a few seconds, McNeill's impudent retort registered, the Indian made a lunge. McNeill's booted foot came up like the business end of a catapult, crashing into the Indian's chin, cracking the jaw.

The Indian was game, despite just having been kicked literally head over heels. He lunged again. This time McNeill deftly, almost effortlessly, grabbed the assailant by the right wrist and underarm and, using the attacker's momentum, threw him into a high arc that ended with a thundering crash on a table that crushed into kindling.

The Indian was conscious enough to realize he was in great pain.

McNeill bent down and said, "Look, chief, with just a bit more twist I could've broken your back or killed you. Now, why don't you catch your wind then go back to the reservation or wherever else you call home, okay?"

The Indian paused, then gave a grunting nod.

McNeill turned and moved toward the bar, awestruck customers clearing a path for him.

Addressing one of the pop-eyed barmaids, he said, "Miss, my name's McNeill. Do you have a message for me from Miss Mimi Revere?"

Maxine, the name indicated on the crammed T-shirt, quickly and nervously rifled through a few notes in a can.

"No, sir, ain't no message here for John McNeill from anybody."

McNeill pointed at the telephone. "That thing come with a phone book?"

"Yes, sir," Maxine said, fishing a dog-eared directory from under the bar.

McNeill flipped to several pages, took a pad and pencil from his blouse pocket, and made some notes.

Going back to Crazy Louie, he asked, "Could you stick with me a little while longer, Louie? I'd really appreciate it if we could talk."

"Yeppir, Colonel," Crazy chirped. "Got the rest of the weekend off, what with lookin' for your daughter. Besides, I'd like to know what you done to do what you done to that big buck."

"Thanks, and call me John, okay? Let's move out."

# ELEVEN

LibertyAire Internal Memo #104 / 93

Dear Employees:

In the past two weeks, as you may have noticed, LibertyAire has implemented a series of advanced security measures. These include new picture and fingerprint identification cards, new plastic key cards coded for restricted admission to specific areas of the facility, more armed guards at points at ingress and egress as well as at highly sensitive divisions within, additional patrols with canines, strategically placed television cameras for total monitoring, and state-of-the-art fence electrification to virtually preclude unauthorized intrusion.

These prudent steps, and others which will follow and of which you will be informed, are designed to minimize prospects for industrial espionage, protect employees and the surrounding populace, and enhance opportunities for obtaining government and commercial contracts that demand utmost confidentiality.

Your cooperation is appreciated.

Homer Platen
Vice President / Human Relations

LibertyAire Internal Memo #105 / 93

Dear Employees,

Effective tomorrow, night-shift activity involving the unloading and transshipment in Sector S-T is terminated until further notice.

In keeping with corporate policy relating to an informed work force, this is to advise that the product we were storing and transshipping nightly in Sector S-T was hydrochloric acid, or HC1. It is a solution of the gas hydrogen chloride in water that produces a strong, highly corrosive acid. It has numerous and potentially lucrative commercial applications, such as in the processing of ore, in the cleaning of metals, and as a reagent.

The prior nondisclosure surrounding this tentatively temporary activity was attributable solely to competitive consideration, a factor that LibertyAire is confident you will understand and appreciate.

Your cooperation is appreciated.

Homer Platen
Vice President / Human Relations.

John McNeill and Crazy Morgan sat in the office of the White Grizzly Motel, Morgan tipping back his black and beaten Stetson, McNeill remembering to adjust his wristwatch to conform to Montana time.

The colonel referred to his notes and dialed the telephone.

"Montana Highway Patrol, Sergeant Curtis speaking. How may I help you?"

"Sergeant, my name is John McNeill. I'm calling to see if there's been any development concerning the disappearance of my daughter, Amy."

"Sorry, Mister McNeill, nothing's come up yet. Have you tried the sheriff's office? Want his number?"

"I have it, thank you."

He gave the sergeant the motel's phone number and dialed again.

"Sheriff's office, Deputy Whitcomb."

McNeill identified himself and the purpose of his call.

Another "sorry," with the deputy adding, "Say, aren't you the guy who whomped Big Chief at The Skull Popper?"

"That what he's called?" McNeill replied. "It was a case of self-defense. I'm sure you've been told *that*."

"You did a number on him, McNeill. Not to worry though. Won't be any charges pressed. Sorry about your kid. We'll keep looking. Unfortunately, she's not the only one we're trying to find. Couple newlyweds and a pair of climbers have turned up missing within the past few days. Feel like we're on a treadmill."

McNeill left his number and dialed again.

"Forest Service, Ranger Tatum."

After McNeill repeated his purpose, Tatum said, "Been over the area several times. Only thing we found was a bullet-riddled grizzly, a big sucker. I was in Nam. Looked like that bear was stitched with an AK-47 or an M-16. We're hauling him out. Coroner wants to do an autopsy."

McNeill asked for and received the coroner's name, address, and telephone number, as well as the coordinates of the bear discovery.

He checked his watch. "Still more than an hour before LibertyAire lets out."

Crazy looked at the wall clock and nodded. "Take us less than a half hour to get there. Hafta wait for the gang to come outside. Security freaks."

"Let's go to my room," McNeill said. "I'll grab some pop and we'll shoot the breeze for a little while."

McNeill propped himself against the bed's headboard, Crazy sat on the chair.

"Everybody in Amy's crowd except you seems to work at LibertyAire," McNeill said. "Why not you, Louie?"

"Ain't got the book learnin' for one thing. Other'n that, I like doin' things outdoors. Most of the time, it's odd-job stuff. But lately I been full-timin' it as a laborer on a chink's palace near Lake Magnifique. One of the guys says he thinks he's seen him at LibertyAire. Looks awful old to be workin' anywhere."

"Chink?" McNeill asked, smiling in spite of himself.

"Yeh. Chinaman maybe. Maybe a Vietnamese or Korean. Maybe a Jap. Who knows?"

"And you say it's a palace."

"Fanciest digs I ever seen," Crazy replied, sipping his pop. "Big logs fit so tight they don't even use caulkin'. Oughta be done fairly soon. Workin' two shifts. They tell me they're shippin' in chandeliers all the way from Italy. Landscapin' a gook garden that'd knock your eyes out."

"Know the guy's name?"

"We all calls him Mister Isoru. That's the last name that's showed on the contractor's buildin' permit."

McNeill sat up and wheeled his legs from the bed to floor. He considered intently for a moment, then smiled and shook his head.

"What's up?" Crazy asked.

"Runaway imagination, most likely," McNeill replied. "See, in Japan, for example, persons' names are generally reversed. Instead of John McNeill, I'd be McNeill John.

Wouldn't happen to know the owner's first name, would you, the one that appears in front of Isoru?"

"No," Crazy said, disappointingly, then brightened. "But we could get it off the schematics in the records office."

"Know how to get there?"

"Just minutes away," Crazy answered.

McNeill looked at his watch.

"We still have time to burn," he said. "Nothing to lose. Let's go."

McNeill looked at the schematics an obliging clerk had brought to him at the records office, seemingly in anticipation of a duplication request that would carry with it a tidy fee.

Crazy, who had stopped at a nearby vending machine to buy a Coke, ambled in and looked through some brochures on a high-legged desk, as though he were idling time until he could be waited upon.

McNeill shook his head and distractedly walked out the door, completely oblivious to Crazy's presence.

Crazy followed within a few minutes, catching up with McNeill at the Ford.

"That was an oddball one," Crazy said.

"In what way?" McNeill asked, with a face that was already puzzled.

"Soon as that clerk in there seen you was out the door, she grabbed a phone and told whoever she was talkin' to that he, meanin' you, just left. I made like I was just in there lookin' for one of their handouts, took one, and left. I don't think she figgered we was together."

"Interesting," McNeill said. "Just like the name of your Oriental owner. Unless it's a weird coincidence, it's a guy

I know, and it just doesn't add up. His full name's Takashi. Takashi Isoru. I'll fill you in later. Let's go see the gang."

Amy looked uncomprehendingly at her plush, windowless accommodations. The bathroom was not only brand new but very large, with a shower, which she'd just used, a jacuzzi and whirlpool tub, a wide-mirrored vanity, and a designer-style toilet. Shelves behind the mirrors and under the vanity contained every imaginable feminine bathing product, from shampoos to moisturizers, razors to exclusive perfumes.

The bedroom was at least twenty by twenty, with a king-size bed, antique side tables with matching lamps, a pair of five-drawer dressers brimming with underwear, sweaters, and stockings, and a thirty-inch TV.

The closets were filled with new and fashionable blouses, skirts, dresses, jeans, shorts, and shoes, all in Amy's size.

She had put on fresh underwear and sox, suede moccasins, a short-sleeve blue blouse, and prefaded jeans, after which she had halfheartedly picked over a sumptuous meal that featured filet mignon, medium rare.

It had been wheeled in by a formidable-looking woman, named Gretel, who had absolutely no answers to Amy's entreaties as to what in hell was going on.

When she turned on the TV, she soon discovered that she could not turn to a local newscast. There were numerous books from which to choose, classics to best sellers, and a veritable library of videos for the cassette player, none of which had the slightest appeal under the circumstances.

There was a knock at the door, followed by Gretel's entrance. Two expensively dressed men came behind her.

The woman wheeled the cart away and closed the door, blocking Amy's inquisitive look.

"Gretel been taking good care of you, Miss McNeill?"

"Don't patronize me," Amy flared, her blue eyes flashing. "Who are you guys, and why am I being held in a locked room?"

"My name is Corbin Bates. My associate is Carter Urban. We work for the Central Intelligence Agency. We have to detain you for a while as a matter of national security. You inadvertently happened across a top-secret installation. Ironically, if our guards hadn't heard your screams, you'd be in a bear's belly."

"And pigs fly," Amy retorted. "You just happen to roll aside your fake grass cover, flip up a phony mountainside, have a jet take off, and I'm supposed to believe this dump is top secret? What do you take me for, some hash-slinging imbecile who flunked out of third grade?"

Bates covered a smile. Instead of the simpering, intimidated kid he'd expected, he was being confronted by a nerveless bobcat.

He gave a quick glance at Urban, who seemed similarly bemused, and continued, "The take-off you saw was a monumental mistake, despite the fact that we'd picked up your copter on our radar. The persons involved have been appropriately punished. To preclude any repetition, we're buttoning the place down during daylight hours while the search continues, at least until top secrecy becomes immaterial."

Amy glanced quickly from Urban to Bates and said to the latter, "I think you're a pair of gold-plated liars, two out of the original Three Stooges. I'm kidnapped and just happen to wind up in a suite clogged with outfits from *Victoria's Secret*, amazingly all in my size. For the life of me,

I can't imagine why, but I think your little shell game was a trap. How long are you going to play this stupid game?"

"It's not a game, Miss McNeill," Bates replied coldly, "As to your question, ours is relatively a very short-term mission. Extraordinarily so. We'll be able to release you in several weeks at the most."

"Several weeks!" Amy exploded. "What about my poor father? He's a widower and I'm his only child. He'll be desperate not knowing what's happened to me. And my friends? Why should they be left dangling in the wind?"

"I'm really sorry for them and you," Bates said, not all that convincingly. "Our nation's security has to be the top priority. Try to be patient. We'll make your stay here as comfortable as possible, within obvious limits, of course."

"Your solicitude is really touching," Amy said between clenched teeth. Then her beautiful blue eyes narrowed, her lips turning into a malign half-grin.

"Want to let me in on the humor?" Bates inquired.

"For me, not for you, Mister Bates," Amy replied venomously. "I know my dad. He won't rest until I'm found. When that happens, I wouldn't want to be either one of you creeps. He'll tear you apart with his bare hands. You don't know him!"

"We know all about your father," Bates replied, with an undecipherable look at Urban.

Urban glanced from Bates to Amy and said, with a flicker of apprehension, "True."

To which Amy commented, "My God, it can talk, even if it's only a single, one-syllable word."

John McNeill hugged Mimi hard and kissed her cheeks the minute she emerged, wide eyed with delight, through LibertyAire's guarded employee gate.

She was so emotionally wrapped up that, tearfully, she gave Crazy Louie a big hug, too. Crazy took it with a shy, silly look on his face.

"Oh, John, I never could've believed you'd make it here so fast," she slobbered, returning to hug him again.

"Couldn't wait a minute to see you, Little Red Riding Hood," McNeill said softly, "and to get to the matter at hand," he added in all seriousness.

While McNeill and Mimi talked, Crazy ran through the parking lot, collecting Swede Olsen, Jerry Duncan, Jeff Curry, and Mike Smith, informing them of the colonel's arrival. Jerry and Jeff, who'd been working the night shift, had been called by Crazy to meet there.

They ran to the pair and took turns introducing themselves enthusiastically. All except Jerry Duncan, who began with what started out as an agonized apology.

McNeill waved it off, saying, "Look, I'm not into the business of recriminations, at least not where Amy's friends are concerned. So, let's throw away the sack cloths and keep our eye on the only rabbit that counts, finding Amy."

Now the enthusiasm was unanimous.

"John, guys," Mimi intruded, "let's say we go to Amy's and my cabin and pound out a plan. We can pick up pizzas on the way."

After they'd squatted outside the cabin and divvied up the pizzas, McNeill summarized his almost fruitless contacts with the various law-enforcement agencies.

"Picked up one piece of information that may be helpful," he said. "They found a grizzly shot to hell by automatic fire, supposedly in the vicinity where Amy fell into a black hole. They're doing an autopsy. I've got the coordinates where the bear was nailed."

Handing a note to Mimi, McNeill said, "Give the medical examiner a call, will you, to see if there's been any determination. If not, try again tomorrow."

Mimi nodded, took the note, unspeakable dread covering her face.

Turning to Jerry Duncan, McNeill said, "Would you and your chopper be available yet today so we can take a look at where the bear went down?"

"Yes, sir!" Jerry responded. He was not only itching for a professional's guidance, he was also in awe, as were the others, of Crazy's description of the Big Chief encounter.

"For one thing, Colonel. . . ."

"Call me John, please," McNeill interrupted. "Everybody, okay?"

"For one thing, John," Jerry continued, "my dad's given me carte blanche with the copter, until Amy's found. And, not that it'd make any difference, because I'd take the time off anyway, but, " he waved a couple sheets of paper, "I'm off night work. Night or day, though I'm ready to fly any time you are."

"May I see those?" McNeill asked.

Jerry handed him LibertyAire memos 104 and 105.

McNeill read the first.

"Like you said, Louie, they're security freaks. You'd think they were guarding Fort Knox. Interesting."

He read the second memo.

"How much hydrochloric acid passed through?" McNeill asked.

Jerry looked at his night supervising partner, Jeff Curry, for confirmation.

"Four thousand fifty-five gallon drums," Jeff replied.

McNeill whistled softly. "That's a pile. Had this kind of volume in the past?"

"Not that we know of," Jerry answered. "Rumor is, they're getting ready for some mine reopenings or expansions, maybe in Butte. Anyway, aside from the acid, the biggest prior shipment was in our old standby, thiodigylcol. We peddle it mostly to our ballpoint pen customers."

McNeill's face hardened. "Did Amy know about these shipments?"

"She knew about thiodigylcol," Mimi replied, "but none of us knew about the acid until that memo came out. Why do you ask, John? Before you answer, let me tell all of you about something you're going to write off as women's silly intuition."

"Go ahead, Mimi," McNeill said flatly.

"She denied it, but I told Amy she had a funny hunch about something and that her latest hike was more than just a gambol in the boonies."

McNeill paused for a long moment, his gray eyes set in deep concentration. The gang looked at each other wonderingly.

Finally, he asked, "Any of you have a notion as to what you get when you mix thiodigylcol with hydrochloric acid?"

They shook their heads.

"Mustard gas."

# TWELVE

Jerry Duncan and John McNeill sat in the latter's new accommodations at the King of the Hill Motel, a plush contrast to the White Grizzly.

More important, it had a telephone, to which McNeill was attaching an answering system, and a motel fax machine.

"Sure we'll be able to use your father's chopper this afternoon?" McNeill asked as he rummaged through his suitcase.

"No problem," Jerry replied.

McNeill extracted a penlight, K-bar marine knife, binoculars, and a zoom-lens camera and stuffed them into his newly purchased backpack, together with a canteen and small package of plastic sandwich bags.

"I'm going to make some quick calls, then we'll hightail it for a look-see," McNeill said, as he punched numbers on the phone, adding, "I want to take advantage of the dry weather."

"Top," he said into the phone to Master Sergeant Oscar Riley, "take notes. Get hold of Lieutenant Colonel Hardaway and tell him to yank chains at the CIA, DOD, Commerce, and OSHA. I need a fast read on an outfit called LibertyAire Chemical Company, from day one. Also, an update on one Takashi Isoru. I'll give you my phone and fax numbers. If their info is sensitive, have it sent overnight via Fed Ex. Here's my address."

76

McNeill punched another number and said, "Colonel John McNeill for Senior Agent Manfred Schmidt."

After a ten-second pause, he continued, "No, Manny, she's still missing. Might have to ring you and your FBI chums in on a suspected kidnapping, one of several hereabouts recently.

"Put that on temporary hold. Right now I need a Code One on a telephone call originating today between fifteen thirty and fifteen thirty-five from this number."

He recited the number, added his phone and fax numbers and motel address, rang off, and punched out another call.

"Jake," he said to his jogging pal at Quantico, Colonel Jake Coltrane, "I'm working with a short fuse. Amy's still missing and the plot's thickening. Put on your scrambler."

After a two-second pause, McNeill continued, "You still testing that loud stuff you were telling me about?"

"Flying colors as of today, bunkie," Coltrane replied. "It's better or worse than we imagined. Far more potent than semtex. Its unofficial code handle is C Ten Power."

"This is going to sound off the wall, but can you ship me ten pounds of that punch, some of those new blasting caps, and a couple of the battery-operated detonators?"

"Jesus, John, you want to blow up a mountain?" Coltrane asked incredulously.

"I'm trying to hit all the bases, Jake, and I've only just rounded first," McNeill responded. "If I'm forced to use it, I'll guarantee you it'll be in the national interest. Can do?"

There was a pause. McNeill glanced at a completely baffled Jerry Duncan.

"Okay," Coltrane finally resumed. "As principal investigator, I've got a free hand. I'll take some of it out to the proving grounds, blow up half, and ship you the other half, in one package. The blasters and detonators I'll send each separately. I'll also include some basic instructions on detonation. Remember, you can mangle or sculpt the stuff any way you want and it's safe. It only turns nasty when you insert the caps and tune the trigger. Good luck. Now give me that address."

After he complied, McNeill asked Jerry, "Do you have a metal detector?"

Jerry nodded.

"Good. Let's bring it along."

"Nice spread," McNeill said as Jerry maneuvered the helicopter over his father's ranch and headed west. "Not interested in being a rancher?"

"Not really," Jerry replied. "In one respect it's all right, I suppose. If you're an owner, you can make it hand over fist. But it's at the expense of nearly everyone else. The cowboys work twelve hours a day, seven days a week, for eight hundred dollars a month and room and board. It's part of a tradition. Break the pattern and you're a pariah.

"Another thing that kind of rubs me the wrong way is what I call the screw-the-taxpayer syndrome. An awful lot of cattle is allowed to graze on federal land for what amounts to peanuts."

"So, what do you plan to do with yourself?" McNeill asked.

"Stay with LibertyAire just long enough to finish my MBA, then try my hand at managing property, maybe in the Big Sky area. Lots of money rolling in, from folk who'll want someone to keep a sharp eye on their spreads. Much as I love Montana, though, I'd do a one-eighty if Amy said so."

McNeill smiled but let the comment pass as he peered through his binoculars.

"Y'know," Jerry continued, "it's odd, but I recall Amy doing the same thing you're doing now, looking to her right side with binoculars, as if she were trying to catch a glimpse of something she'd seen on a previous flight."

"Did you see anything out of the ordinary?" McNeill asked.

"Nope."

"Any roads down there going through the forests?" McNeill persisted, looking at his pilot.

Jerry shook his head and said, "May I ask you something?"

"Shoot."

"What's your take on the potential of mixing those two chemicals at LibertyAire to produce mustard gas, and just how bad is mustard gas?"

"It could be nothing or it could be something," McNeill answered. "Two hundred twenty thousand gallons of anything is a bunch, let alone hydrochloric acid. It could've been transshipped to legitimate outlets, as claimed, or manifests could've been doctored at either end to disguise the trail. I'm going to try to find out.

"As for mustard gas, it's been around since the Germans started using it in World War I. There are many nastier gases, but dichloroethyl sulfide, or mustard, is bad in any company. Appropriately, in concentrated form, it even smells like mustard and has an oily brown color.

"It causes victims to throw up, become temporarily blind, and suffer horrible blistering. A gas mask can prevent it from causing internal injuries, but it can seep through layers of clothes, even boots, and play hell with your skin. It can also lie around for days and still be destructive. Ironically, when the British returned the favor and lobbed some mustard of their own, one of the casualties was Adolph Hitler."

"My God, what could be worse than that?" Jerry asked.

"Mustard was only one of about fifty gases used in the First World War," McNeill replied. "Chlorine was a real killer. Phosgene is invisible, smells like new-mown hay, and was ten times deadlier. One-fourth of America's casualties in that war were gas-related. Another thing, you can throw a double whammy with gases. Use one, like chloropicrin, to penetrate masks and cause nausea. Use another, like phosgene, to kill when the mask is removed so the victim can throw up. We have stuff today that's infinitely worse."

"We've arrived," a very sober Jerry Duncan announced.

When they landed, McNeill strapped his camera around his neck and began scanning the landscape with his binoculars, while Jerry began walking in a widening circle around the copter.

Jerry stopped suddenly and shouted, "I think this is where the bear went down."

McNeill ran to the spot that revealed a wide swath of coagulated blood covered with flies and ants.

"Get the metal detector, will you," he said and, pointing toward the stream, "let's mozey back and forth to the edge of that water."

Jerry strapped on the metal detector's headset and began descending, criss-crossing twenty-five yards to either side.

As he approached a thick bush roughly twenty yards from the stream, he stopped and said, "Got something."

Before McNeill could race to his side, Jerry had pulled from inside the base of the bush a cloth-covered canteen.

McNeill took it excitedly, examined it carefully, and said, "This is Amy's, a gift from me. Look, see the initials 'AM' I stenciled on the bottom. Those people who've been searching this area remind me of one of my dad's classic observations. They couldn't track an elephant through ten feet of snow if its throat was slit. Good find, son. Let's keep going toward the stream."

As they neared the water, rainless days and a scorching sun had combined to preserve the mud-baked footprints of a bear and a person with small feet.

McNeill photographed sets that indicated the person had approached the stream and then turned away from it, the bear paw prints following.

"She and the bear must've spotted each other at the same time," Jerry said. "Then she started running, dumping her canteen and pack."

Looking uphill, he added desperately, "But where could she have gone for protection? That nearby stand of trees couldn't hold a kitten. And even a track star can't outrun a grizzly."

McNeill searched the mountainside.

"Come on," he said, heading, uphill, "I think I see something that could've been a hiding place."

"Doesn't add up," Jerry said. "Why would these big logs be here when all the others nearby are scrawny?"

"Maybe somebody wanted a bunker here, for whatever reason," McNeill replied.

"Look," he added. "These are claw marks, big ones. A bear couldn't crawl through the opening, but a person could. And somebody or something had a fire going between the logs."

"Get a load of this," Jerry said, holding up several strands of green fiber. "Amy was wearing a green outfit when I brought her here. These could've come from her sox."

"Great!" McNeill said, as he put the fibers in a clear sandwich bag. "We'll scour the chopper. Maybe we can get a DNA matchup."

McNeill peered through the opening with his pen flashlight.

"Poke your detector in there," he told Jerry.

Jerry inserted the device as far as he could. Instantly, there was a rapid crackling sound.

"There's heavy metal in there and it has nothing to do with music," he said.

McNeill reacted by shedding his pack and wiggling through the log opening.

Inside, he began probing with his K-Bar knife at the end wall of the cave.

He soon struck something metalic sounding. When he sliced downward, he discovered that the dirt was layered over a tarpaulin. More cutting and pulling revealed the outline of a barrel, then another, then still another. One was unmarked, the other bore the inscription HCL.

"There are fifty-five-gallon drums in there," he told Jerry after he crawled out. "Looks like a storage dump. No idea how many, but somebody's gone to a lot of bother to conceal what's apparently hydrochloric acid and something else that's not identified."

Jerry was speechless. Then, looking down past McNeill's shoulder, he said, "Company coming."

McNeill whirled to see the figures of two men approaching unhurriedly, grabbed for his camera, adjusted the zoom lens, and took two pictures. He cased the camera, put it in his pack, put on the pack, picked up Amy's canteen, and leaned nonchalantly against a log.

The visitors looked hardbitten in their camouflage suits, one carrying a rifle, the other a double-barrel shotgun. The heavier of the two had a dark complexion and dark eyes accented by a black stubble. His partner was taller, slim, pale blue eyed, and almost albino white, including the hair that shown on his forehead beneath a tilted black cap.

"Prospectin'?" the dark one asked with a forced smile.

"Yes," McNeill responded. "Hunting?"

"Yeh," the dark one answered. " 'Bout ready to call it a day. We was just headin' back to our tent, over that way," pointing in a westerly direction.

"No luck, apparently," McNeill said.

"Nothin'. You guys do any good with that fancy divinin' rod?"

"Nope. Still looking for the pot of gold at the end of a rainbow." McNeill smiled.

The dark one glanced noncommittally at his expressionless companion.

"We was lookin' for a canteen I stashed in a bush near here. That one you got in your hand looks mighty familiar. Didn't happen to find it with that detector, did you?"

McNeill looked sternly at Jerry. "Matter of fact, we did," he answered. "Here, take a closer look. If it's yours, it's yours."

McNeill handed over the canteen. The recipient smiled. "Got lucky, Vic. Found it. Much obliged. Well, guess we'll be movin' on."

When the hunters departed, Jerry said, excitedly, "They're lying through their teeth. I caught your signal, but I still don't know why we didn't jump them."

"Because they're armed and we aren't and because I want to find out more about them," McNeill said. "I suspect they're guards, perhaps under surveillance, maybe carrying distress beepers. True, I could've taken them out by myself. But what the hell would we do with them? I could've tortured them enough so they'd betray their mothers. But we could've come up with a dry hole. Sure, they're liars, but are they implicated in Amy's disappearance? Every move I make has to be calculated. My daughter's life could well lie in the balance. Let's go home."

# THIRTEEN

Back at his father's ranch, scanning the helicopter's interior with a magnifying glass, it took Jerry Duncan only twenty minutes to announce to John McNeill, "Found something."

McNeill looked up to see Jerry holding a thread of green fiber, which he immediately compared to the thread contained in his plastic sandwich bag.

"I'll run it by a lab," McNeill said, "but it sure looks like a match to me. Good eye, Jerry."

"I can get a friend at LibertyAire to do the lab analysis," Jerry said then added, "Amy must've hid from the bear in that cave. When she crawled out, she got nabbed by the person or persons who riddled the grizzly. Maybe because they figured she stumbled into the drums you discovered."

"Not likely," McNeill said. "That tarp and mud-covered wall wasn't disturbed until I started digging. Besides, if they were that antsy about their hidden drums, why weren't we nailed?"

"Possibly because they were too scared of another disappearance in the same neighborhood," Jerry persisted. "If we became no-shows, what with the flight log I filled out, this place'd be crawling with searchers. Sooner or later they'd have to figure that cave and its unusual log cover ought to be looked into."

"Point taken," McNeill acknowledged. "Let's get to Mimi and see if she's found out anything.

On the way to the cabin Mimi shared with Amy, McNeill saw an all-night pharmacy that advertised one-hour film development.

"Pull in there," he told Jerry.

He went to the film counter and was gratified to see a clerk on duty.

"Soup this for me, will you, son," he said to the teen-age clerk. "If you can get me eight-by-ten blow-ups of the faces of the two men on the film, and do it in an hour, you get this," McNeill added, flashing a fifty-dollar bill.

"You got a deal, mister," the kid responded eagerly, grabbing the film.

Mimi was smiling widely on the cabin porch as McNeill pulled up.

Jerry got out first and asked, "Why the giggle?"

"An hour ago I talked with the coroner," Mimi replied, "a real nice lady. She said the only thing in the bear's stomach was an undigested fish, a brown trout. Not a trace of human flesh. What a relief!"

"That's great news," McNeill said. "Anything new from the law-enforcement agencies?"

"No," Mimi said. "They're starting to get a little paranoid. Amy included, they have five people they're looking for and they haven't a clue. They told me they're widening the search area and using bloodhounds. Newspaper and TV reporters have been driving them batty."

Crazy Louie was waiting in a rocking chair in front of the King of the Hill Motel when McNeill returned.

"Hungry?" McNeill asked.

"Always," Crazy answered with his thin, Cheshire cat grin.

As they waited for their sandwich and coffee order at the next door diner, The Garden of Eatin', McNeill, as he'd done with Mimi, reviewed the day's events.

He took out two photos from a large envelope, handed them to Crazy, and asked, "Know these birds?"

"Yep," Crazy said, frowning. "Them's the Rayder brothers. Vic's the tall whitey. Ernie's the pudgy one. They're guards for LibertyAire. Them the ones you come across when you was out lookin' for Amy?"

"Yes. What else can you tell me about them?"

"Few days ago they bought a brand-new Jeep Grand Cherokee and was flashin' a fat wad at the Skull Popper. Said they'd hit it big in Vegas, at the twenty-one tables, no less. Anybody knows 'em knows they ain't got the brains to pour piss outa a boot, let alone outwit a card shark."

As they were eating, a matronly-looking office clerk from the King of the Hill approached, handed a note to McNeill, and said, "I noticed you pull in."

"Thank you," McNeill said, handing her a five-dollar bill.

Crazy smiled and said, "Kalispel clerks ain't used to that long a tip for that short a ride."

"Small investments can sometimes bring big returns," McNeill said, scanning the note.

"I have to make a quick call," he told Crazy. "See you tomorrow."

In his room, McNeill spoke into his phone. "Colonel John McNeill for Lieutenant Colonel Thomas Hardaway."

In a second, Hardaway was on the line.

"Sir," he said, "I have a quickie rundown on LibertyAire. Thought it better to call on a scrambler than fax or mail it."

"Appreciate the speed, Tom. What do you have?" McNeill asked as he took out a pen and pad.

"It's privately held, incorporated in nineteen seventy-two. Steady growth, with sales last year hitting one point two billion. Heavy into pesticides, insecticides, textiles, and pens.

"Has a lucrative subsidiary, LibertyAirePlane. Consists of some four hundred crop-duster planes nationwide.

"Has thirty-two hundred employees, most of them in Kalispel, including the air arm and twelve sales offices from New York to California.

"The firm gets a clean bill of health from Commerce. DOD says no problem in compliance with prohibitions against foreign shipments of toxic chemicals."

"Who bankrolled the outfit?" McNeill interrupted.

"Sir, the big money was apparently pulled together by a Carlos Carto, who allegedly fled Cuba in nineteen sixty-eight. Until his death from a heart attack last year, he was chairman, president, and CEO. Now his wife, Dolores, is chief honcho. She also came from Cuba in sixty-eight, at the age of twenty, which makes her forty-five years old now. She was naturalized in August of seventy-eight.

"She's very low profile," Hardaway continued. "Nobody seems to know what she does besides run her shop. However, State says she's logged a lot of trips to Havana, under hardship visitations to family members."

"Interesting," McNeill said and quickly added, "Wait one, Tom. There's somebody at my door."

When he opened it, he was greeted by the matronly motel clerk who smiled and handed him a folded fax sheet.

McNeill noticed her name tag.

"Thank you again, Molly," he said and handed her another five-dollar bill.

87

The fax read, "To: John McNeill c/o King of the Hill Motel, Kalispel. Caller I.D. Takashi Isoru, Kalispel exchange. Unlisted. Regards, Manny."

Speaking into the phone, McNeill said, "Sorry for the interruption. What else have you got?"

"Something of a new twist, Colonel," Hardaway replied. "A big-time CIA germ guy by the name of Takashi Isoru retired, pleading bad lungs. The cloak-and-dagger boys are fairly tight-lipped about it, but evidently Takashi got a ton of dough to go with LibertyAire. Part of the separation was tied to his finishing up research on simulants for very poisonous weapons. Also, the guys who were Takashi's controllers at Fort Detrick, named Bates and Urban, also signed on with LibertyAire. The agency implies they're to keep an eye on Takashi. Other insiders say it's more a matter of their making a pricey career shift. In short, Takashi was their primo meal ticket and, allegedly, still is. That's about it, sir."

"Fast work, Tom," McNeill said. "I'm going to play another hunch. Fax me a complete list of locations for those crop-duster planes. Take a copy to Bill Turnbull at the FBI. Tell him I want all of those places put under twenty-four hour surveillance because I'm beginning to smell chemical sabotage and I need time to sort the thing out. I'll be in touch."

He hung up, got long-distance information, and punched a phone number.

"Caesar's Palace," a voice answered.

"I'd like the suite of Mister Tomas Napoli, please," McNeill said.

A gruff male voice answered, "Yeh?"

"My name's Colonel John McNeill. I'd like to talk with Mister Napoli."

"He's a busy man. What d'ya wanna talk to him about?"

"Look, sonny," McNeill shouted, "if you're stupid enough to brush me off, I'm going to be able to hear your screams all the way from Vegas to Montana, as Tommy Napoli nails your balls to the wall."

McNeill could envision a beefy hand covering the other phone's speaker and that a hasty message was being relayed.

Within seconds an excited voice yelled, "Colonel McNeill! Jeez, this is great. Like a bolt outta the blue. To what do I owe the pleasure?"

"Nap," McNeill said, "I'm in one very tight bind. My daughter's been missing in Kalispel, Montana, since Sunday. That's where I'm calling from. I can't go into all the details right now, but I'd like you to check on a couple of suspicious characters."

"Anything. Anything," Napoli said.

"Thanks. I'm going to fax you a couple mug shots, with descriptions. They're of two guys who claim they made a recent killing in Vegas, enough to buy a new Jeep Grand Cherokee and still flash a thick wad of dough at the local slop chute."

"That'd be about fifty G's," Napoli said. "That kinda moola goin' to a pair of rubes would not go unnoticed. I'll dub the photos around to all the casinos. Dealers who can memorize the play on five decks of cards will be able to remember those mugs, that is, if they showed up here. I'll also have all the hotel registries checked. Ain't nothin' goes on in this town I can't find out. It's a cinch. Have it for you tomorrow. What else can I do?"

"I need some hardware, Nap."

"Name it, Colonel. I can outfit a battalion."

"An automatic pistol with a silencer, a boot Derringer, a high-power rifle with a night scope, and ammo for all of them."

"You got it. I'll have it flown to you in my private jet. Be there tomorrow mornin'. Where you stayin'?"

McNeill told him.

"It'll be right at your door. Sorry as hell to hear about your daughter, Colonel. Best o' luck. Anything else you need, just tell me what it is. Still owe you big time."

John McNeill got up at seven, after a fitful night of half-sleep. He showered and shaved, hoping the activity would help clear his mind. It didn't. His head was reeling from one unrelated recollection to another, out of a day that had been jammed with jarring revelations.

He put on gray slacks, a blue sport shirt, and shiny black loafers.

"Anything for me, Molly?" he asked at the motel office.

"Yes, sir," she answered, "you got this stack of fax papers and these three boxes."

McNeill reached into his pocket.

"Oh, you don't need to tip me, Mister McNeill. This one's on the house," Molly said with a big smile.

"Take it anyway," McNeill insisted handing her a five-dollar bill. "What're friends for?"

He took the materials to his room.

The faxes were Lieutenant Colonel Tom Hardaway's lightning-like response on the location of LibertyAire Plane's crop dusters. The list was broken down state by state, from one coast to the other, with the heaviest concentration in the Midwest.

At the top of the first page, there was a handwritten note that read, "Turnbull's on board for surveillance. T.H."

McNeill put the faxes in his suitcase, then opened the packages. The largest contained the ten pounds of C 10Power, shaped in a square. It looked like pink plumber's putty.

One of the smaller packages held a dozen slim, three-inch-long cylinders, sparkling in a variety of iridescent colors. The other contained three twist-type ballpoint pens and a miniature audio cassette, with a taped-on note, "Play me. J.C."

McNeill pressed the play button and heard the familiar voice of Jake Coltrane.

Here are your toys, John. The putty is completely benign until activated. You can shake it, bake it, sculpt it, paint it, or whack it with a hammer. No problemo.

The cylindrical blasting caps have similar virtues and, like the putty, are non-detectable with even the most sophisticated scanner or bomb dog. They each have an inch-long, pin-size antenna at one end where you can see a tiny indentation. Pull the antenna up with your fingernails when you want to activate. If you change your mind, simply push the antenna down.

The ballpoint pens do triple play, a la James Bond. First, they can actually be used to write. Just twist the pen and start composing. Second, to turn them into detonators, pull off the clip, unscrew the top cap, and turn the serrated wheel until a red dot aligns with the white arrows on either side. They're pre-coded to the blasting caps, so all you have to do to detonate is press the exposed top down. They're effective up to one thousand yards. Give yourself plenty of distance. We're dealing with Godzilla.

The third feature of the pen / detonator is in turning it into a one-on-one weapon. To do this, you twist the pen to the writing position, pull off the clip, aim the writing end, and press the opposite end, the one with the screw on top still in place. It will fire a poisonous projectile up to fifty feet. Obviously, as with a pistol, the closer the target, the better.

Burn this tape. Good luck, Jake."

McNeill put a cigarette in his mouth, then decided against lighting up. He put it back in the pack, which he tucked into his shirt pocket, gathered up his materials and placed them in the trunk of his rented Ford.

As he walked to the Garden of Eatin', McNeill saw a gleaming black stretch limo parked outside the diner.

Inside, the place was packed, mostly with men in ten-gallon Stetsons, Levis, plaid shirts, and cowboy boots, chowing down on the day's special of gravied smoked pork chops, home fries buried under ketchup, eggs, ranch toast, and coffee, with additional carafes at each table.

Seated at one of the booths that bordered three of the diner's walls were two men sipping coffee. Both seemed as out of place as if they'd just landed from Mars.

One was very large, dark, and rough enough looking to appear a natural for his cauliflowered ear. He wore an expensive dark gray business suit.

The other, short and trim, also had a dark complexion, with jet-black hair combed straight back, adding prominence to his thick eyebrows and penetrating dark eyes. His light gray suit looked straight out of Giorgio Armani's. When he raised a hand to mask a whisper, he displayed diamond cuff links and a pinky ring that matched the diamond stud in his black tie.

McNeill nodded as if he'd solved a momentary puzzle and made his way past the red-and-white checkered tables to the booth.

"Nap?" he asked.

The man in the exorbitant outfit jumped up, exclaimed "Colonel McNeill!" and hugged his long-ago hero.

"I'd'a known ya anywhere," Tommy Napoli blubbered. "Except for the gray hair, you ain't changed a bit since you saved my buns back in Nam in sixty-eight."

Turning to his burly companion, Napoli said, "Carmine, meet the swellest man God ever put into shoe leather, Colonel John McNeill. Colonel, my business associate, Carmine Archangelo."

The big man stood with an embarrassed half-smile, extended his hand, and said, "An honor to meet you, Colonel."

"You wouldn't be the telephone receptionist I spoke with yesterday, would you?" McNeill asked, smiling.

"He is," Napoli answered for his companion. "And you was right, Colonel. If he'd cut you off, he'd'a been singin' with the castrati, associate or no associate."

McNeill sat next to Napoli.

"Didn't expect to see you playing delivery boy, Nap, but it's nice to see you in any event," he said.

"Can't tell ya what this means to me," Napoli replied. "Any news of your kid?"

"Nothing."

McNeill filled them in on some of the things he'd been up to regarding the search, but not on any of the more sensitive aspects.

"Jeez, I wish I could do more," Napoli said. "Anyway, we brung what you asked for. It's in the trunk outside. Carmine here's an expert on the hardware. He'll show you how everything works when we get outta here. As for the guys you wanted me to ask around about, you can take it to the bank that they didn't win nothin' in Vegas, last week or last year.

"Thanks," McNeill said. "Let's go to my room. I'd like to familiarize myself with the stuff and hit the road ASAP."

# FOURTEEN

Amy McNeill, dressed in a pink-and-white spandex outfit, pedaled hard on the stationary bike. She'd requested it and had been surprised when it was delivered to her room the same day.

She had difficulty figuring how long she'd been a captive. Was this Thursday, Day Six?

There were no windows to reveal sun or moon. The stone-faced matron, Gretel, refused to answer any questions.

Amy suspected that, when all but one of the lights in her suite went off, it was nighttime. When they went on again, after a long interlude, it was daytime. She alternated her sleep and activity accordingly.

Often, she was close to or beyond tears. Exercise offered a much-needed diversion and boost to her tenuous morale.

After an hour of biking she switched to doing a series of pushups, situps, and other assorted calisthenics.

Bored, nonetheless, she started examining the many videos stacked alongside the big TV and VCR. She was intrigued by one that promoted the benefits of Tai Chi, for both contentment and martial arts.

She plugged it in and soon became fascinated by the soothing music and the ritualistic exercise movements of the slim, bespectacled Chinese instructor.

Following his directions, Amy discovered that, after no more than a half hour of seemingly undemanding gyrations, she was beginning to feel as though she'd been run through a very different kind of ringer.

By simulating the holding of a large ball going from left to right, by lifting and lowering her arms just so, by doing the same with her legs and torso, her whole body eventually responded to new challenges. The payoff was a sense of relaxation she'd never before experienced. The turning movements also allowed her to look more intently at the Charles Russell paintings that lined her walls, and which she loved.

Her eyes roamed other parts of the room, her mind considering for the thousandth time what piece of furniture or lamp cord might be employed as a weapon to dispatch Gretel and attempt an escape. Amy felt confident she could subdue the large woman with a smashing blow or cord strangulation, perhaps as she was opening the door. But then what? Was she likely to face immediate recapture? The workouts helped greatly in calming her down and re-thinking.

After the soothing effects wore off, however, she became agitated and psyched up to try almost anything.

Her heart, Amy discovered for the first time, was turning toward unbridled hatred devoid of fear.

John McNeill answered the phone call in his motel room as he was changing into his fatigues.

"Jerry Duncan, John. My lab friend says the green fibers are a perfect match. No margin of error."

"Thanks," McNeill acknowledged. "As they say, the plot thickens. Catch you later."

He hung up and inserted the two-shot Derringer in the top of his boot, covering it with a pant leg, tucked the three pen/detonators in a jacket pocket, behind which he strapped the holster with the silencer automatic pistol. He recalled Carmine's expert instruction that the silencer was only effective for about nine shots.

As he was molding clumps of C 10Power into fist-size balls and inserting the blasting caps, the phone rang again.

"This is Maxine," a voice said. "They just come in and ordered breakfast."

"Thanks," McNeill said, and hung up.

He threw some elk jerky and cheese and cracker packets into his backpack, along with the makeshift bombs, ammo clips, some short lengths of rope, binoculars, map, compass, and camera, and put his K-bar knife sheath through his belt.

McNeill checked the trunk of his rented car, lifting a blanket top to reveal the rifle with its telescopic night lens.

Satisfied, he closed the trunk and drove the car to the Skull Popper Saloon, parked and waited.

A half hour later, Vic and Ernie Rayder emerged from the saloon, got into their new Jeep Grand Cherokee, and headed up 93. McNeill followed them.

The Jeep slowed when it came to a sign with an arrow indicating the direction to Lake Magnifique, and turned left onto a dirt road. McNeill waited a minute and resumed the pursuit, punching on his trip odometer.

The road was a narrow one-way, heavily forested on both sides, with turnoffs every few hundred yards, to allow one car coming or going to pull aside so the other could pass.

As he proceeded, occasional breaks in the foliage provided McNeill with short glimpses of a magnificent log home situated with a commanding view of a lake. The house, he calculated roughly, had to provide ten thousand square feet of living space under its pentagoned roof. All around its perimeter was a wide porch, and around that, sculpted gardens now being bathed in sprinkler mist.

A hundred yards farther on, McNeill encountered a gated stone road that led to the extravagant house. He stopped, peered through his binoculars, saw no sign of the Jeep, and kept going.

He glanced at his trip odometer, which indicated he'd traveled twenty miles since leaving the highway.

After another ten miles, his way was blocked by a swivel gate bearing a sign warning that he was approaching private property and that trespassers would be prosecuted to the fullest extent of the law.

It seemed pretty obvious to McNeill. After referring to his map and compass, he concluded that Jerry Duncan had been wrong about there being no road to the area where Amy had vanished.

He pushed the gate aside, drove through the opening, replaced the gate, and drove on.

As the trip odometer registered thirty-five miles, McNeill saw, roughly one hundred yards ahead, a widening of the road. On either side was a parking area, covered by camouflage netting.

McNeill looked overhead and directly back, and saw that the overhanging trees would completely obliterate the road from above. The parking lot camouflage would complete the deception.

He inched ahead slowly, found an opening to his right, and drove his car to a spot twenty yards in, to where high grass virtually obscured it from the road.

He put on his pack, retrieved the scoped rifle from the trunk, and worked his way back carefully toward the road, using a branch to rework the bent grass back to a semblance of its former appearance.

McNeill ran quickly along the dirt road for approximately ten yards, ducked back into the foliage, and crouched his way nearer to the parking area.

He soon counted fifteen vehicles, including a bright red Jeep Grand Cherokee.

Immediately beyond the lot was the corner outline of a camouflaged, two-story building, the first level twice as high as the second. Above it was a continuation of the netted cover that originated with the parking space.

McNeill ducked low as a door opened and Vic and Ernie Rayder came out, each with an AK-47 on his shoulder, each wearing a cartridge belt loaded with clips.

They headed in the opposite direction, away from McNeill and along the side of the building.

McNeill circled wide to the right, keeping the pair in view as they walked unhurriedly along a building that appeared to extend approximately one hundred yards. At the end of it, a wide camouflage net descended, like the site of a mountain, to a base that, from McNeill's perspective, looked like a swath of artfully contrived artificial turf. A road to and from nowhere or a concealed landing strip to a disguised hangar? Whatever, he told himself, it all somehow involved his daughter.

His eyes followed along the turf's length to the other end, where another disguised side appeared. McNeill snapped a sequence of pictures, then noticed the Rayders climbing the mountain until they were twenty or so feet atop the fake siding, where they leveled off to take a look around.

Given the exceptional coverage provided by the forest, McNeill pursued the brothers rapidly, his face contorted in anger.

From behind a boulder, McNeill could see the Rayders look inside the cave that gave Amy temporary refuge, then walk away, glance around the periphery, and appear to head back to their base.

McNeill drew his silencer pistol and held it high in the air to accentuate the loudness of its being cocked.

The Rayders heard it and turned quickly in McNeill's direction, unshouldering their rifles.

"Hello, boys," McNeill said evenly, as he leveled the pistol at them. "Drop your weapons. I want us to have a little, friendly chat. One false move and the only sound you'll hear is your quick screams. This, unless you don't recognize it, is a silencer."

The Rayders, thoroughly shaken, tossed their rifles aside.

"Now, come to me," McNeill demanded. "That's good enough. Stop. Throw your cartridge belts away. Stand with your hands knotted over your heads."

"What the hell you up to?" the dark-faced Ernie demanded.

McNeill fired one soundless round into the questioner's upper leg. He cried out in terror as he fell to the ground. His white-haired brother, Vic, gasped, eyes staring in disbelief as he looked at Ernie's blood-soaking trouser.

"Christ, man," Ernie pleaded while grasping his shattered leg, "what the hell'd we ever do to you?"

"If he doesn't know," McNeill said, looking at Vic Rayder, "I'll bet you do, you rotten lying son of a bitch."

The brothers exchanged terrified looks.

"Lying?" Vic stammered. " 'Bout what?"

McNeill fired again, this time into the platinum blond's leg. Instead of a scream, he gave an animalistic groan, and dropped in shock.

"Have I got your full attention?" McNeill asked.

They nodded vigorously in dumbfounded, saucer-eyed wonder.

"You've been shooting your big mouths off," McNeill continued in an ominously soft voice, "about how you made a killing in Vegas. I checked. You weren't anywhere near the place. You lied."

Pointing at Ernie Rayder, he said, "You claimed that canteen I gave you was yours. It belonged to my daughter. If you weren't such a stupid clod, you'd have noticed her name inscription on the cover. You lied."

"You said you were hunting the day we met. You weren't. You were guarding, among other things, the barrels that are hidden in the dugout behind those logs."

The Rayders looked at each other, sweat streaming down their faces, not knowing what to do to placate the madman confronting them, glancing furtively as more blood oozed from their legs.

"Eenie, meenie, minie, moe," McNeill said with a sadistic leer as he waved the ghastly pistol from side to side, "what should I shoot, Vic's knee or Ernie's toe?"

"Please, mister," Ernie begged, "we'll tell ya anything you wanna know. Just don't shoot no more."

"Where's my daughter? If you don't answer in three seconds, pop goes my weasel."

"She's down there," Vic shouted, pointing at the fake mountainside.

"What's down there?" McNeill pressed.

"A hangar and a building with offices and labs."

"Who owns the place?"

"LibertyAire."

Turning to Ernie Rayder, McNeill asked, "Why did you want my daughter's canteen?"

"Our boss said we was to bring back anything that we could that belonged to the kid. We seen her carryin' it before the grizzly cornered her."

"Who's your boss?"

"Mister Bates."

"What does Bates want with my daughter?"

"We don't know," Ernie answered, "honest to God."

"What's under that stretch of fake grass?"

"A landing strip," Vic answered, "for jet airplanes. Least that's all we ever seen come and go. Been buttoned down lately, what with the searchers and all."

"What about those other four missing people, the newlyweds and the climbers?"

The brothers looked at each other.

"Time's almost up," McNeill threatened.

"We snatched 'em," Ernie replied. "Mister Bates told us where we could get 'em."

"That's how you came into your alleged Las Vegas winnings, right?" McNeill persisted. "How much were you paid?"

"Fifty grand," Vic said.

"Be back in a minute," McNeill said, as he picked up their rifles and threw them as far as he could.

He went to the cave opening, pulled up the antenna on one of his C 10 Power balls, and tossed it to the rear.

He returned to the wounded duo and tied their hands tightly together with some of the rope he'd brought in his pack.

"Our field outfits are almost identical," McNeill noted, "except for the caps. Yours have a thin metal band going around the peaks. Why?"

"It's to identity us as the door," Ernie answered. "You press it against a slit the size of the peak under the door window."

"What other ID is required?"

"Just a plastic key card we rub through a slot at the door."

Turning to Vic Rayder, McNeill demanded, "Where's yours?"

"Left jacket pocket."

"That's it, that all I need to gain entry?" McNeill asked.

The brothers looked at each other and nodded.

"Why do I get the idea you clowns are holding out on me?" McNeill continued, as he took Vic's cap.

"Pay close attention," he said, extracting a pen from his pocket. "See this? Looks like a run of the mill ballpoint pen, doesn't it?"

They nodded, puzzled.

"Well, now," McNeill resumed, "when I spin off the top, like so, and twirl the little wheel underneath, it turns into a detonator, effective up to a thousand-yard radius. All I have to do is press down and explode my bombs, one of which is in the cave."

The Rayders looked stunned and frightened.

"When I get down there and try to get inside that building, I'll have this detonator all primed and ready to go. If I encounter any trouble at all, I detonate and your little piece of earth goes to hell in a handbasket. If the blast doesn't kill you, the explosion will release what's in those fifty-five gallon drums. That will release an ocean of mustard gas. Miles downwind, it would only mean horrible blisters and terrible nausea. Here, you'd be as blistered as a side of beef forgotten on a spit. You dig?"

The Rayders nodded, then glanced at each other with a smug look of triumph.

"A thumbprint's gotta be used and matched with the plastic card," Vic Rayder confessed.

"That everything?" McNeill inquired.

"Yep, that's it," Ernie answered.

McNeill got up quickly and kicked Vic Rayder senseless. He took out his razor-sharp marine knife and cut off half of Vic Rayder's right thumb as easily as though he were slicing through soft butter, squeezed out most of the digit's blood, and put it into a plastic sandwich bag.

Ernie looked as though he was going to pass out.

"Stay alert, Ernie," McNeill invited. "Never can tell when you might have to wriggle away from a bear or rattler. When Vic comes around, tell him I hope he has a nice day."

# FIFTEEN

Takashi Isoru detested LibertyAire's hidden facility. The trip to it from his lake-view mansion was long and arduous over dirt road. Except for his personal accommodations and those of the captives, the place was as unappealing as any he could imagine.

There were no windows. All lighting was artificial. The soundproofing produced an eerie effect. Walls and ceilings were painted a dull white. Floors were uniformly covered with dark green carpeting. The only features he considered welcome were the building's air conditioning and ventilation system.

Even in his expensively furnished office, Takashi's *wa*, or serenity, was disturbed. To be sure, one entire wall was filled by an aquarium, the others with floor-to-ceiling murals with Japanese motifs, accented by displays of various samurai swords.

On the highly polished hardwood floors rested low-level tables, numerous colored satin pillows, scatter mats of thin bamboo, and heavily lacquered urns. Comparatively plush but totally inadequate to one with his sensibilities.

Takashi contented himself in the knowledge that his visits were near an end. The great operation was about to begin.

His servant girl, Akita, appeared in a kimono to announce the arrival of his guests.

"Show them in, then serve the tea," he ordered.

Takashi, also attired in a kimono, stood to greet his subordinates, former CIA agents Corbin Bates and Carter Urban.

As they approached, he bowed and noted cynically that both were shod in polished cotton slippers.

"I'm so pleased you could join me," Takashi lied, gesturing toward the pillows flanking the tea ceremony table.

"We're delighted to be here," Bates lied back.

As soon as Akita poured their tea into small, round, and elaborately painted cups, Bates and Urban sipped carefully.

"Excellent," Bates pronounced.

"Delicious," Urban added.

Takashi smiled in acknowledgment, then asked, "The prisoners?"

"The four subjects just completed their final physicals," Bates answered. "Per your instructions, they're confirmed as being in great shape. Granted, the newlyweds aren't delighted with their honeymoon accommodations. Nor are the mountain climbers with theirs. But we told them it's only a matter of a little more time and we'll be turning them loose. I didn't say it'd be in Gillette, Wyoming."

"Excellent," Takashi said.

Turning to Urban, he asked. "And the little blond woman?"

"Feisty and frustrated," Urban replied. "Fortunately, she's turned into an exercise freak. Does all sorts of calisthenics, and seems to have taken a fancy to Tai Chi. All told, she's holding up well."

"Good," Takashi said, adding, "and you, gentlemen, how are you holding up?"

"I'm quite satisfied, Professor," Bates responded. "You had us over a barrel. Anything happens to you, your secret colleagues spill the beans and Urban and I are road kill. The invitation to join your team was like a life buoy. We clear the table, dump the Company, and are free as birds."

"And, the pay's great," Urban interrupted, "and the risk manageable. If we're successful, we're all in clover forever. If we flop, we've all got a guaranteed sanctuary. It's win, win, as I see it. What about you?"

"Oh, I'm very pleased," Takashi responded. "As I'm sure you surmised, my alleged excuse for taking a medical separation resulted not from disability but from the cooperation of a physician with an itchy palm. I'm in excellent health for being only seventy-eight. My lineage is very formidable, so much so that I fully expect to enjoy another thirty years.

"As for Montana, it is a delightful contrast to the insufferable D.C. area, and I have an exquisite home and a quite generous employer.

"Of preeminent importance," Takashi continued, "our projects help me avenge somewhat the destruction the United States heaped upon my beloved country and fellow countrymen. Herding innocent civilians into concentration camps, Hiroshima and Nagasaki, an interminable occupation, all and much more have tormented my soul.

"Admittedly, I would have been executed after Japan's surrender had I not been a unique expert in chemical warfare experiments on human beings, not only on the battlefield but in a controlled laboratory environment. It is a supreme irony that all my learning during and after the war has now put me on the threshold of threatening the United States with unprecedented consequences. That is the perspective of a true son of Nippon. Yours is a different perspective. It is your country we are about to threaten with potentially great harm to countless citizens you swore to protect."

"I won't lose any sleep over it," Bates said. "Way I see it, it's going to be the government's call as to who does or does not get zapped. You've guinea-pigged humans, so has our side. Some of it, like the Negroes who suffered from untreated syphilis, and dangerous army tests involving civilians, have gone public. A lot more hasn't. Every power-house has gotten away with murder. It's all samey same. When you get down to it, to mix metaphors, it's dog eat dog and every man for himself."

"Interesting as well as brutally incisive," Takashi said. "I appreciate the directness you employ in arriving at the bottom line, as you often put things.

"Well, now," Takashi continued, "I see it's nearing the hour when our special guests will be arriving. More tea?"

Vic and Ernie Rayder, after long and painful exertion, finally freed themselves of their bonds.

After strenuously rubbing their wrists, they promptly took off their pant belts and applied tourniquets to their bloody legs.

"I ever get the chance, I'm gonna kill that lousy son of a bitch," Ernie swore.

More concerned with his own hide than McNeill's, Vic shouted, "Forget him. What the hell we gonna do?"

"I'm in a bad way," Ernie said. "Gotta get a branch or somethin' to hobble on 'fore we can get anywhere."

"Whadaya say I use our cellular phone and call for help?" Vic asked.

"You outta your mind," Ernie stormed. "He never bothered to search us to see if we had one. He doesn't give a damn. We blow his cover and he blows us to hell."

"Then what?"

"We drag our butts down to the parkin' lot and get outta here as fast as we can."

107

McNeill sighted through his infrared telescopic lens, checked his watch, then resumed scanning all around the grounds below.

It was nine-thirty and darkness was beginning to thicken. There were no lights to draw the attention of aircraft.

There were no dogs or guards to be seen. McNeill speculated that the Rayders' watch, which began at two in the afternoon, would conclude at ten, when they would be relieved. That gave him half an hour to finish his surveillance and break in.

He moved quickly, ducking behind boulders and trees, stopping only long enough to rescan the area.

It took only minutes to circumvent the phony grass and make his way along the length of the building to where the security door was located.

Every twenty paces, McNeill stopped to cram a bomb at the base of the wall. He made five such stops.

When he came to the end of the building, he surveyed the parking lot. It was still nearly full as before, only this time there were also two limousines.

McNeill examined the door. Black light bordered three different-sized boxes. One was a narrow rectangular slit obviously meant for insertion of the cap visor. Another indented into the door about two inches, with an opening like that of an automatic teller machine. McNeill rummaged in his pocket for the plastic card key and placed it just outside the slot receptacle to confirm his assumption.

The third box surrounded a flat button slightly larger than a man's thumbprint.

McNeill cursed himself for not getting the sequence in which the identification steps were to be taken.

As he pondered the question, he could hear the sound of one or more vehicles approaching.

He had to make a fast choice: wait for the newcomers and burst in behind them as they were being admitted, or follow his hunch that the IDs were to be applied as they were arranged, left to right.

McNeill inserted the edge of the cap visor and immediately heard a buzzing sound. When he inserted the plastic card, another buzzer sounded. He took Vic Rayder's thumb from the bag and pressed it against the button. A third buzz went off and the door opened.

Inside, the room was completely dark. Before the door could close automatically, McNeill tore off his pack and used it as a door stopper.

He unshouldered his rifle and aimed its infrared night light to his front. Ten feet away, behind a glass enclosure, sat a beefy, frowning guard who was just rising from his chair and fumbling for his pistol.

The guard groped gingerly to come out of the enclosure and, like a sleepwalker with outstretched arms, headed uncertainly toward the door.

When he reached it, he felt along its edge until his hand touched McNeill's pack.

"What the hell?" he mumbled as he released the pack and closed the door. Lights went on instantly.

When he looked up, he saw McNeill with the barrel of his silencer one foot from his head.

"Give me your pistol, handle first," McNeill ordered. "Now give me the pack and get behind your glass door."

The open-mouthed guard complied immediately.

Inside the glass cubicle, McNeill said, "Company's coming. I'm going to be under your desk. Play it cool, just like nothing's happened. If you give me away, I'll blast your cajones from here to Tucson. *Comprendez?*"

The guard bobbed his two chins repeatedly and sat in his swivel chair.

Moments later three successive buzzing sounds were heard, the lights went out, and the door opened.

"Hi, guys," the guard said when the door shut and the lights went back on.

"How's it goin', Elmo?" a voice asked.

"Anything happen'?" another voice inquired.

"Duller'n mud," Elmo replied.

McNeill could hear the sounds of lockers being opened and shut.

"See ya," one of the voices said as the door was being opened, again bathing the room in darkness.

When the door shut, resuming the lights, McNeill asked "Who were they?"

"Night guard shift," Elmo answered.

"Why didn't they ask about the guards they're replacing?"

" 'Cause they probably seen their Jeep and figgered they was just around the place doin' somethin'," said Elmo, shrugging.

"What's behind that door?" McNeill asked, pointing to an entrance directly behind the glassed cubicle.

"Mister, I plain don't know," the guard answered. "All I'm supposed to do is press a button, here, and that lets anybody with a special ID badge go through. That don't include us guards. They don't even give me a visitor's roster to check off. You ain't gonna kill me, are ya?"

"Not if you behave. I want you to give me your cap and plastic key, then I'm putting you outside. I strongly advise you to get in whatever vehicle you're driving and get the hell out of here. There's a good possibility I'm going to blow this place to kingdom come. You stick around to tell your pals and you could all go sky high."

# SIXTEEN

"The days dwindle down to a precious few, eh, my old friend?' Fidel Castro asked of General Juan Juarez as the two sat on the large patio under a glorious evening sky.

They were at El Presidente's north coast, heavily guarded villa, Castro in his usual fatigues, Juarez in white dress uniform. A gentle breeze wafted the smoke of their expensive cigars. Only in his choice of outfit was Fidel Castro average. Everything else was la creme de la creme, most definitely so in his selection of the world's choicest tobacco.

"That is so," Juarez answered. "Today's final experiment is more pro forma than anything, mostly to create a respectful impression. In any event, we're in a solid position to forge ahead."

"Do you think the Americans will think we're bluffing?"

"No," Juarez replied. "Not after their experience with the missile crisis. They know incontestably that it was Khrushchev who wilted and threw in the towel and that you were ready and willing for a showdown. If your first name were Nikita instead of Fidel, it would be a far different confrontation. Besides, the Russians weren't protecting their own land but that of a disposable partner, Cuba. You made Kennedy very nervous. That's why he tried so hard to have you killed."

"There are two other important considerations that will weigh heavily on the Americans," Castro said, gazing at the star-filled sky. "They realize, as do I, that I'm not getting any younger. For all they know, my temperament could be suicidal on a grand scale because my hard-earned revolution is being devastated by their infernal meddling.

"It's almost funny," Castro continued with a rueful smile. "The Americans dole out billions to prop up a former Soviet economy that went broke trying to maintain nuclear supremacy and threaten the world. Then they turn around and award most-favored-nation trade status to a China that killed thousands of their troops in Korea and which is contemptuous when it comes to human rights. Yet, I am the pariah. Talk about inconsistencies!

"Yes, Uncle Sam is shrewd enough to recognize the gambler in me. They've backed me into a corner and will concede that, given sufficient retaliatory resources, I would be inclined to say to hell with the consequences. What difference does it make if they kill us slowly, as they're now trying to do, or vaporize us in a flash?"

Looking at his thick cigar, Castro said somberly, "It would be a supreme tragedy, of course, on both sides. The slaughter of the innocents," then with a wink, "including the best cigars and baseball players in the world, and many of the best boxers. Let me know as soon as we receive the score from up north."

"FBI Deputy Director Turnbull on the line, sir," Lieutenant Colonel Tom Hardaway's clerk advised.

"Hardaway, sir."

"Tom, I need to talk with John McNeill as soon as possible," Turnbull said. "I've called and left faxes, per the numbers you gave me, but there's no response. My neck's on the line. I've got to come up with something fast for the director that's more than just a hunch, to maintain all the agents I've assigned to monitor LibertyAirePlane."

"Sorry, sir," Hardaway said, "but I'm as much in the dark as anybody. He hasn't called and I haven't been able to draw a response, either."

"I've had LibertyAire checked out six ways till Sunday," Turnbull said, "and there's really nothing obvious in the analysis to wave storm signals about. And our guys in the field haven't been able to detect any monkey business at the company's crop-duster airstrips. What's your feel?"

"Colonel McNeill's no nervous Nellie," Hardaway answered. "If he says he's worried about something, I take him dead seriously. It's not at all like him to ignore important messages. I'd guess he's too hot on a trail to get the word back or...."

"Or what?" Turnbull demanded.

"Or he's been killed, incapacitated, or taken captive," Hardaway replied.

"Damn, wouldn't that be a turn," Turnbull said just above a whisper. "I'm going to assign a beefed-up team to scour Kalispel. Meantime, you hear anything at all, anything, get on the horn. We've got to shake this thing loose."

# SEVENTEEN

McNeill pressed the door-opener button from within the glassed enclosure, heard a rapid clicking sound, and saw the entrance to the building's interior open an inch width.

He shouldered his rifle, opened the door wide with the tip of his silencer, and stepped in crouched low, both hands on his weapon.

It was a long, narrow hallway, brightly lighted, revealing doors on either side approximately fifty feet apart.

He tried one of the door knobs. Locked.

He stepped back two paces and fired five rounds around the knob, then kicked it hard. The knob fell off as the door opened.

Inside stood a large woman in a pinstripe maid's uniform. Her mouth was open, her eyes wide with wonder.

"Keep your mouth shut," McNeill demanded as he quickly surveyed the room. It was a small suite, modestly furnished, much like that of a mid-range motel.

"Who are you? What are you doing here?" she stammered.

"I'll ask the questions," McNeill snarled, as he continued. "Any hesitation, any suspected lie, and I'll start blowing away your arms and legs."

The big woman fell to her knees, arms extended beseechingly, tears of terror streaming down her cheeks. "Please don't shoot me," she implored. "I'll tell you anything I can."

"What's your name?"

"Gretel. Gretel Hauptman."

"What do you do here?"

"I wait on the, uh, the guests."

"Guests! You mean prisoners, don't you?"

"Yes."

"How many?"

"Five."

"One of the prisoners is a curly-haired blond named Amy. Where is she?"

"At the end of the hall, in Suite A."

"You'd better have a key to open her door."

"I do, sir, I do!"

"Get up and get it. Try to make any kind of a signal and you go straight to hell."

The woman, crying and shaking, struggled to her feet and pulled a large key ring from a wall peg.

McNeill motioned her to lead the way.

As they walked the length of the hall, McNeill noticed what appeared to be two small, half-concealed TV cameras, one to each side.

"Stop," he ordered. "From here, how do you get to the wall on the other side of the building?"

"At the end of this hall, you go left all the way to the end," Gretel replied.

"Stay where you are," McNeill said, and retreated several paces.

He aimed carefully and fired at one of the TV lenses, then at the other.

At the sound of the quiet burst and the shattering, Gretel staggered, grabbed for her chest, and leaned against a wall.

"You pass out on me and I'll take your key ring and leave you for dead," McNeill barked.

She gulped for air, recovered, and stumbled on.

When they reached Suite A, Gretel fumbled the keys and inserted one in the door. It opened.

McNeill pushed her roughly inside.

"Hi, sweetheart," he said, almost melting with joy at the sight of his daughter.

Amy moved in shocked slow motion and disbelief.

"Dad!" she squealed, when the apparition proved real, and she ran to embrace him.

They hugged hard and long, McNeill rocking his beloved Amy but never taking his eyes off Gretel.

"Somehow I knew you'd find me," Amy said through copious tears. "It's the only thing that kept me going."

"Heaven and earth, honey," McNeill whispered. "Heaven and earth."

Turning to Gretel, he ordered, "Go into that bathroom, shut the door, and remain perfectly quiet."

When the door was shut, Amy asked, "How in the world did you ever find me, way out here in the boonies?"

"Later, sport," McNeill answered. "They're undoubtedly on to me by now. We've got to make tracks and get to the other side of the building. God, what a relief to see you're okay."

"They didn't harm me. I got good food and I was at least able to get in some decent workouts. But I never got a hint on what's going on."

McNeill went to the bathroom door. "Stay in there, Fräulein Hauptman, until somebody comes to release you. You come out on your own and you could be walking straight into a bullet."

"Yes, sir," a frightened voice said from behind the bathroom door.

"Amy, do you have an outfit that can cover your entire body?" Everything?"

"I've got jogger clothes with hoods and gloves, and scarves that'd cover my face."

"Any goggles?"

"Yes, a couple sets. I alternate using them when I turn on the suntan lamp."

"Get them," McNeill said. "I'll take one, you the other. Get into that hooded jogger outfit and bring along the scarves."

He kept watch on the door as Amy quickly changed.

"Let's go," he said, as he led the way out of Suite A and handed her his pistol.

As they came to the end of the hall, McNeill peeked around the corner and broke into a trot.

Again, he noticed a pair of TV cameras and stopped, Amy almost bumping into him.

He reached for the pistol she carried and fired twice, destroying the cameras.

"Gee," Amy said, "it hardly made any noise. Just a sort of sput."

McNeill winked, replaced the silencer adapter with the spare in his pocket, handed the pistol back to Amy, and signaled to keep going.

When they reached the opposite wall and turned the corner, McNeill unscrewed the top off one of his three ball-point pens, moved the serrated wheel until a red dot appeared between two arrows, and pulled off the clip. Carefully, he placed the pen back alongside the other two.

"We've got to find an exit from this dump, hon," McNeill said. In a whisper he added, "Either that or I'm going to have to blow half this building to smithereens. Where we are now, we'll be well shielded from the blast. After that, though, we'll have to run through the debris like demons, get to my car, and roar out of here."

"I'm all for blowing the place up," Amy said bitterly.

"Kinda thought you would," McNeill said, smiling.

As they hurried along, a voice resonated through a hidden loudspeaker.

"Colonel and Miss McNeill, please listen carefully," the voice said.

"All exits are sealed and guarded. There is no escape. Please put down your weapons. No harm will come to you. We have to talk on a matter of great urgency. Once we talk, we guarantee your release. It would be very regrettable if we were forced to use tear gas."

McNeill looked frantically backward and forward. He put an index finger to his lips and whispered to Amy, "Don't say anything about my blowing the place up."

She nodded, as her eyes widened.

"How do we know you'll keep your word?" McNeill shouted.

"Realistically, you have no alternative," the loudspeaker voice replied. "Come on, Colonel, your daughter's been well treated. We could've gassed you at almost any time. Be reasonable. All we ask is a little cooperation."

McNeill shrugged, placed his rifle, cartridge belt, and knife on the floor, and motioned to Amy to drop the pistol.

Soundlessly, a panel in the wall opened and out stepped two tall, sharp-eyed men in combat fatigues, each bearing a heavy pistol.

After one of the guards retrieved the McNeills' weapons, the other felt around McNeill's boots until he found and extracted the Derringer. He then frisked the McNeills, ignoring the ballpoint pens.

McNeill glanced at Amy, a surprised look on his face.

One of the guards gave an after-you gesture.

McNeill and Amy stepped through the panel opening into a short, yard-wide corridor, at the end of which another door opened.

There to greet them were three men and a woman, in a large room with Japanese furniture and appointments.

"Thank you for coming," one spoke up, "I'm Corbin Bates."

"Late of the Criminal Intelligence Agency," McNeill said with heavy sarcasm.

He turned to the other American-looking man and added, "And you must Carter Urban, another CIA turncoat."

Urban nodded with a smirk.

"As for you," McNeill said, as he looked at the elderly Oriental male, "why, if it isn't my old pre-Desert Storm buddy, Takashi Isoru. Still dreaming up newer and more terrible ways to afflict mankind, Professor?"

Takashi chuckled. "I see you've lost none of your astuteness, Colonel. I told my colleagues your mind works with remarkable speed and precision. Ah, but forgive my bad manners. Allow me the honor of presenting Señora Dolores Carto, the chairman and president of LibertyAire.

"My pleasure, Colonel," the señora said, extending her hand. "I've heard so much about you. Miss McNeill, "she added with a nod and perfect teeth smile.

McNeill shook her hand and immediately regretted his reflex reaction. He withdrew his hand quickly.

Still, he was almost stunned by Dolores Carto's beauty. The LibertyAire dossier revealed her to be in her forties. With jet-black hair swept in a bun, large brown eyes, and flawless olive complexion, all accented by a white silk pantsuit and sandals, she looked barely in her thirties.

"Chanel Number Five?" McNeill asked her.

"Yes," she answered with a delighted smile. "As the professor said, you are uncommonly perceptive."

"I can tell the difference between an expensive perfume and, for example, mustard gas," McNeill said and added, "Did he also tell you I can, on occasion, be a very dangerous and impulsive guy who disdains false civilities and prefers to cut to the chase? Speaking of which, why did you snatch my daughter, and what the hell's going on here?"

Amy came to her father's side and hugged his waist.

"As you wish, Colonel McNeill," Takashi replied. "Answers to all your questions will evolve in a sequence of steps, each in its proper order. We will now take the first step."

Takashi waved a hand and one of the guards pressed a button. A wall panel moved to a side and exposed a large one-way window.

"Come, look," Takashi invited.

The group gathered at the window and looked down on four stark white bedroom-size apartments, each outfitted with a cot, toilet, wash basin, chair, and one occupant, three of whom were young males, the other a young woman. All were dressed in hospital-type gowns. Their ceilings were of plain glass. All of the inmates paced nervously.

Outside each compartment was a two-person team of what appeared to be a doctor and nurse, or perhaps medics, seated at a table covered with a variety of medical paraphernalia and a pair of gas masks.

"The newlyweds and climbers who suddenly vanished when Amy was kidnapped?" McNeill asked.

"Yes," Takashi replied with an appreciative smile.

"Dad," Amy said, with alarm in her voice, "what are they going to do to those poor people? They look frightened to death."

McNeill clenched his jaws but did not reply.

Takashi pushed a wall button that opened another panel and revealed a wide display of pint-size jars behind thick, bullet-proof glass.

"Colonel," he invited with a gesture, "do you recognize any of these labeled contents?"

McNeill walked closer to the display and said, "If they are actually what the labels indicate, they're natural toxins."

"Correct," Takashi said, "and can you identity their potential applications?"

"What is this, a Poisons One-o-One exam?" McNeill answered angrily.

"Please indulge us," Takashi said soothingly, "your perceptions are vital to this whole process."

McNeill glared at him and reexamined the jars.

He pointed and said, "That one, the Columbian frog, is the source for batrochotoxin. The Chinese cobra is convertible to cobrotoxin. The South American rattlesnake, to crotoxin. The jellyfish, to seawasp toxin. Do I need to continue this inane recitation? I recognize them. They can be translated into biological weapons."

"Excellent," Takashi said as he clapped his bony hands. "These," he added, "are only a portion of a much larger supply representing a virtually total range of chemical and biological weaponry.

"Some," he continued, "I've had the honor of being able to convert into simulants. That is, the simulations have the same devastating effects initially, but the result is not deadly, as would be the originals. Now, for the demonstrations."

He walked back to the window overlooking the four separate compartments and said, "Come."

Señora Carto turned away and walked toward a table. "I believe I'll have a nice cup of coffee," she said as she looked pointedly at Amy and added, "Would you care to join me, Miss McNeill?"

Amy shook her head and joined her father at the observation window.

"Four compartments," Takashi said, "four subjects, four different simulant demonstrations. The simulant amount is impressively small, three ten-thousandths of a diluted liter. Observe."

He signaled to Carter Urban, who moved a switch. Down below, a red light went on outside each of the compartments. The eight attendants donned gas masks.

There was no other sign. No sound or color of gas.

Within seconds, the captives began shaking convulsively. They fell to the floor, writhing. Although the sound did not carry to the observers, the victims were obviously screaming during brief breaks in their projectile vomiting.

"You sons of bitches," McNeill shouted, clenching his fists, his face a mask of sheer hatred.

Bates and Urban moved quickly away from him.

Amy turned sheet white and walked away crying. Señora Carto went to her, offering a solicitous hand.

"Stay away from me," Amy screamed, "you black widow."

"Regrettable but necessary," Takashi said.

He nodded at Urban, who threw another switch, which turned off the red lights and turned on ones colored green.

Immediately, the eight medical personnel entered the four compartments and began ministering to the comatose victims.

"They'll be coherent in approximately four hours," Takashi explained, "and fully recovered in about thirty-six hours."

"Why the horror show?" McNeill asked with vivid disgust.

"To demonstrate our unique capabilities," Corbin Bates replied.

"But why am I, specifically, the witness?"

"Because of *your* unique capabilities," Bates answered. "Your credentials are impeccable. A doctorate in chemistry, an internationally recognized authority on chemical and bacteriological warfare, and a much-decorated war hero, to boot. You cover all the bases for us, McNeill."

"So, I've observed. Now what?" McNeill demanded.

Bates looked at Takashi and then at Señora Carto.

"I believe the time is appropriate," she said.

Bates motioned to Urban, who went to and opened the door that led into the room.

Two men entered, one large, the other of somewhat less than average build.

"I don't believe introductions are necessary, are they, gentlemen?" Urban purred.

Carmine Archangelo nodded.

"Sorry as hell for the inconvenience, Colonel. But, like I said, you'd find your daughter and she'd be honky dorry."

McNeill looked flabbergasted.

The speaker was Tommy Napoli.

# EIGHTEEN

"Special Agent James Parker on line one, sir," the secretary to FBI Deputy Director William Turnbull announced at his office in Washington, D.C.'s J. Edgar Hoover Building.

"Give it to me round by round, Jim," Turnbull ordered.

"Sir, we swept the area with McNeill's mug shot. Found a waitress at a local saloon who said Mac tipped her to inform her when a couple of local goons, the Rayder brothers, showed up. Said she's sure Mac followed them and that they're employees of a chemical outfit named LibertyAire.

"We checked their employer. They hadn't turned in after yesterday's shift. We combed the area and found them in a hospital. Both had gunshot wounds, which they initially claimed were the result of accidents. One had a heavily bandaged face and was minus a thumb. He couldn't talk. His brother said Mac had kicked him silly when they told him he needed three IDs to gain entry to a remote, camouflaged building that covered, among other things, three jet aircraft. The talkative brother said they'd told Mac three items were needed to gain entry to the building, a metalicized cap brim, a plastic card, and a thumbprint."

"Christ on a crutch," Turnbull said. "McNeill cut off the guy's thumb after popping their legs?"

"Apparently so, sir, after admitting they'd supposedly rescued Miss Amy McNeill from a bear attack and brought her to their remote building. We have to assume Mac went into the building to look for his missing daughter."

"Anything else?" Turnbull asked.

"Yes, sir, we checked Mac's calls. He'd contacted a Colonel Jake Coltrane at Quantico. Coltrane says Mac had enough demo to reface Mount Rushmore."

"Oh, my God," Turnbull said. "What could be worse than an unchained Irish marine madman on the loose in Montana?"

"There's also this, sir," Special Agent Parker continued. "Another of Mac's calls went to Caesar's Palace in Las Vegas. A tracer trailed it to a guy named Tomas Napoli. He has hood connections."

"Good work, Jim," Turnbull said. "I'm going to take this immediately to the director. He'll inform the White House and Joint Chiefs of Staff. Meantime, I want you to bring in ninety heavily-armed agents, supplemented by local police and marshalls, and breach this LibertyAire place. Let me take care of the judicial formalities. Also, keep sweating those Rayder brothers until you see drops of blood appearing on their foreheads."

# NINETEEN

"Amy," John McNeill said, "the big one is Carmine Arch-angelo, a flunky for the other one, whose name is Tomas Napoli. I saved Napoli's life in Nam. Ever since, on every Marine Corps birthday, he's sent me a card inscribed, 'Still owe you big time.' Obviously, he has a curious way of expressing his gratitude."

Turning to Napoli, he continued, "I now understand how that guard knew I had the Derringer. He went for it right off the bat, then patted me down."

Napoli, predictably dressed to the nines in a light-blue silk suit and dark tie, excused himself as he passed McNeill to embrace Dolores Carto and exchange kisses on both cheeks.

"You've met my sister. Beautiful, isn't she?" Napoli asked with a prideful grin.

"You're just full of surprises," McNeill answered. "What's next, you going to tell me that gorilla you brought is your son?"

Napoli laughed. "That's a good one, Colonel. Come on, let's everybody sit down and get comfortable. The McNeills deserve an explanation and it might as well begin with me."

When they were all seated, Napoli looked at McNeill and said, "First off, ain't nobody gonna hurt you or your daughter. That's a given."

"Second, to try to explain why you and I are here, I hafta go back to that tour we did in Nam and after I got mustered out. Like most vets who did time in country, I was treated like dirt, called baby killer and all the rest. At first I felt lousy and confused. Then I got mad and started to do a lot of readin'. About how our guys were gettin' purple hearts or comin' back in pine boxes to prop up one of the most corrupt governments in the world.

"Lover boy Kennedy said we had to stop a threat that was ten thousand miles away. What the hell was the Cong gonna do, walk on water? Then that coward Lyndon Johnson suckers J. William Fulbright into sponsorin' the Tonkin Gulf Resolution, givin' him a free hand to kite the slaughter. Only guys with brains and guts enough to yell 'foul' were Wayne Morse of Oregon and Ernest Greuning of Alaska. Fulbright wised up long enough to write *The Arrogance of Power*. He knew he'd been taken for a ride, just like George Romney, when he admitted he'd been brainwashed.

"So, Nixon comes along and the murderin' escalates. We slip over into Cambodia and Laos, and keep bombin' and spreadin' all them pesticides and herbicides, and gettin' infected in return. Every honest book, from *The Pentagon Papers* to *A Bright Shinin' Lie*, shows how we were all suckered.

"But who pays the price? Sure, Johnson ducks out of a reelection bid because he waited too long to find out the party was over. And the rest of the rat pack? McNamara heads up the World Bank, McGeorge Bundy takes over the Ford Foundation, and Dean Rusk gets a hot-shot job as a professor."

McNeill looked at Amy and could tell that much of the monologue was going over her head. He turned his eyes back, intently, to Napoli.

"I know I'm ramblin', Colonel," Napoli continued, "but I gotta get this off my chest so you'll know where we're comin' from.

"See, the first thing I read every day is *The Wall Street Journal*. It's the best record in the country on how the big shots screw the little guy. How they run sweat shops, pay less than the minimum wage, or don't shell out overtime pay. They learned nothin' from the Depression, that when you squeeze wages so much that the little people can't afford to buy. World War Two saved capitalism, but they can't make the connection.

"They use bean counters to figure whether they ought to fix their defective and deadly goods or pay off accident victims. They slap on extra points to mortgages poor people need to afford poor housing. They get the Fed to hike interest rates, cut competition, and throw people out of work. For this they get incredible bonuses or golden parachutes. They scam billions in fraud and theft, pick the public's pocket, and get soldiers killed. And if they're caught with a hand in the till, they almost never do serious time in the slammer."

Napoli took a sip of water.

"Then there's our secret government," he continued. "Colonel, you ever read *Clouds of Secrecy: The Army's Germ Warfare Tests over Populated Areas?*"

"Of course," McNeill replied. "Came out five years ago. Author's Leonard Cole. It documented how the army used chemical tests on an unsuspecting American public."

"Right," Napoli said. "It was cut from the same bolt where they let a bunch of Negroes go untreated for syphilis, where they plunked poor, dumb G.I.s in a desert and exposed 'em to atomic radiation, and where they had 'accidents' that killed crops and animals. Ain't a week goes by without some story about an outbreak of anthrax, or tetanus, or a chlorine spill happenin' somewhere in the world, including our country. Accidents? Bates and Urban here know better. They engineered some of them accidents. I

128

wouldn't be surprised if we find out that the Desert Storm Syndrome is worse than they admit and that it was triggered by a goof-up on our side. Nobody can stonewall like the Pentagon."

"What are you leading to?" McNeill interrupted.

"Just this, Colonel. A poor guy is powerless, just a pawn. I decided long ago I wasn't gonna be poor. I was lucky. I got taken in under my uncle's wing. Sure, it's the rackets, but it ain't any dirtier than most businesses or the Congress that business owns lock, stock, and barrel. To me, it's *a la familia*. The only people you can trust are your own people, or those we control. It's screw or be screwed."

"Okay," McNeill said, "you've explained why you're a hood. What's that got to do with stealing my daughter?"

"Nabbing you outright—and you were the real target—would've set off too many alarm bells," Napoli replied.

"Besides," he continued, "we wanted you to see for yourself what we were up to. So you'd be in a position to size up what we're capable of doin'. I knew you could figure fast, but you really amazed all of us. You got the instincts of a really good hit man. It's why we set those two goofy brothers up, so's you'd track them. They ain't gonna forget you, pal. You play rough. I admire that. Besides, who could be more expendable than those boobs?"

"You took one helluva risk," McNeill said. "I could've gone for backup and stormed this place."

"Not you," Napoli said. "I know you from way back. You don't hesitate. You didn't waste a minute to save my buns or Lieutenant DeGrazia's. Once you learned your daughter was here, I knew you'd be inside pronto. It's in your genes. You couldn't wait to save your baby."

Amy looked up at her father, tears of love and regret in her eyes.

"Another thing," Napoli continued, "your daughter was not only perfect bait, she's also our best hedge against you blowin' your lid."

"Just what *are* you up to?" McNeill demanded.

"Just this," Napoli said. "My sister's husband came to this country from Cuba, where he was close to Castro. He got in by greasing some palms at Immigration. He contacted us. We had money to launder and he had a plan. We bankrolled his chemical business, which is a huge money-maker. We take our cut. We also bought into his idea for Cuba to face off against the United States."

"Cuba in a showdown with us?" McNeill interrupted. Looking around at the others," he added, "You must be out of your minds."

"Quite the contrary, Colonel McNeill," Takashi Isoru said. "You've seen our arsenal. You know we have hundreds of planes across the country that can spew chemical toxins anywhere we wish. From mustard to sudden death, on animals to people. The pilots of those planes are unaware of our little plot. All they do is carry out our instructions. They are completely unsuspecting and, consequently, cannot compromise us when we tell them where to fly and what to spread. To them, they're simply carrying another load of fertilizer or pesticide."

"Each of your planes has been under FBI surveillance," McNeill said. "Checkmate."

"Not at all, Colonel," Dolores Carto interjected coolly. "We are not fools. We've been honing this plan for years and have every contingency to bring it off. We not only have our three jets in the building, we have six others in secret locations, ready to go to work on a moment's notice. Further, we have rocket launchers under remote control, with a variety of chemical mixes, depending on our circumstances and needs."

"What if I don't believe you have these contingencies?" McNeill inquired.

"We are prepared, indeed we are determined, to prove them to you," Takashi answered.

"That's right," Napoli interrupted. "You can pick a spot and we'll zap it with whatever gas you prescribe. You don't wanna do that, then we'll tell you where the hit'll be made and wait for the news reports to confirm it. *Ben trovato*, eh? That's ingenious, in Italian."

"Sounds more like *salto mortale*, or deadly sleep, to me," McNeill rejoined.

Napoli and Dolores Carto smiled resignedly at each other.

"In any event, I'm not playing your crazy game," McNeill continued. "You want to use people or animals for guinea pigs, I can't stop you. Do your damndest. Beyond that, I still can't see where I come in on your suicidal notion."

"You're going to be our and Castro's message bearer," Napoli said. "Everybody in the military will believe you if you tell them we've got the muscle and will use it if we can't cut a deal."

"What's in this for you, Napoli?" McNeill asked.

"We get a hero's welcome in Cuba, carte blanche to set up resorts, build mansions, start air service, later casinos, a central control point for the Caribbean."

"Castro kicked out mob gamblers and prostitution," McNeill said.

"He ain't gonna live forever," Napoli replied. "Meantime, we'll have greased the skids. We'll be well on our way to a great laundry and we'll clean up like Capone."

"What's the message I'm supposed to carry?" McNeill asked. "The bearer of bad news used to get his heart cut out. I'll get my brain cut out for this stunt. Got a note pad?"

As he posed the question, McNeill took one of the un-armed pens from his jacket pocket.

"May I see that?" Bates said, and reached for the pen. McNeill tossed it to him.

Bates twisted the writing end, wrote a few lines on a pad, and satisfied it was harmless, handed it back with the pad.

"May I also make some notes?" Amy asked.

"Sure, kid," Napoli said, "help yourself."

"Dad, may I borrow one of your pens?"

McNeill handed her the pen in his hand and removed the armed detonator pen from his pocket.

"What's your message?" McNeill asked.

Dolores Carto replied, "There are to be no more CIA-type chemical attacks on Cuban soil. The United States must become a signatory to the Chemical Warfare convention."

"Hold on," McNeill interposed. "That requires ratification by two-thirds of the Senate. How are you going to line up that many ducks, when there's so much entrenched opposition?"

"We have patience," Señora Carto replied evenly. "And a certain degree of surgical leverage. Through you, we can let it be known that the states of various bullheaded senators will become prime targets if they remain obstructionists. This, obviously, will be accomplished sub rosa. We don't want self-important senators to lose face unnecessarily.

"Now, if I may continue with our conditions, there are to be no more attempts to assassinate Castro. Your economic sanctions are to be removed, gradually, by quiet executive order. In a year or two, resumption of full diplomatic relations. As recompense for the freezing of our assets and U.S. demands for restitution of property seized by Cuba from various blood-sucking American businesses, we demand ten billion dollars a year over a period of seven years. We'll use part of that sum to compensate for the seized properties, for the sake of U.S. appearances.

"You're providing humanitarian support to North Korea, mostly to keep it from causing trouble. You've made massive concessions to China, despite its sorry behavior. You give billions to the Middle East to placate tyrants. You destroy some dictators and curry favor with others. You can and ought to give Cuba some room to breathe. If not, then it's Armageddon. Castro will not back down, even if you launch an all-out nuclear attack. He's getting old. He's fighting for his people's survival."

"Seventy billion dollars?" McNeill asked. "On the q.t.? How could our government possibly pull off that amount of payoff in seven years?"

"It's chump change," Napoli said. "The CIA budget alone is thirty billion or more a year. It has an oversight committee that couldn't trace a fraction of that loot. Even if a senator or two wised up, they could be convinced to keep their yaps shut, in the interest of good old national security. Aside from the CIA, there's the secret National Security Agency's kitty. And the Pentagon's slush fund. It's all there to be tapped, with only a very few silenced mouths knowing what's really going on."

"All right," McNeill said, "for the sake of argument, let's say the U.S. goes along with your extortion. What about the possibility of a double cross?"

"You tell me, Colonel," Napoli said. "You think any government could survive unlynched if they put their own peoples' lives in a noose? We not only got hidden planes and rocket launchers, we got hit guys who can slip colorless, odorless, poisonous chemicals into waterworks, lakes, rivers, you name it. Say we zap New York, Chicago, and

Los Angeles. Millions of people croakin'. Won't know what hit you until the corpses start showin' up. You saw how little it takes of that phony poison to keel people over. Same for the hard stuff. Only the victims don't recover. Incidentally, just to show you our hearts are in the right place, we're getting ready to release our guinea pigs. A little shaken, maybe, but they're okay, they'll get over it."

# TWENTY

A phone rang. Dolores Carto frowned in apprehension. They were not to be disturbed except for a genuine emergency.

She said, "Excuse me," walked quickly to the phone, and listened to the caller, her eyes widening.

"Tomas," she beckoned to her brother. To the caller she ordered, "Repeat your message to Mister Napoli."

"This is Grimes, in security, Mister Napoli," a voice said. "We've got heavily armed feds in gas masks all around the building. From their ID vests, I can tell they're FBI, ATF, and U.S. marshals. They've got armored vehicles with cannons, and they've been overflyin' with jet fighters. Me and the other guys are goin' out with our hands up. We didn't bargain for any of this when we signed up here as guards. Those feds ain't kiddin'."

Before Napoli could respond, the caller had hung up.

"I'll handle it," Napoli said confidently to Dolores.

"Colonel," he continued, "we gotta put you to work faster than we figured. You hafta go outside and talk a bunch of feds outta bustin' in on us."

"What do I tell them?" McNeill asked.

"Don't go into anything more than the barest details," Napoli cautioned. "They jump our bones, there's Hell to pay. They'll believe you. Tell 'em to back off and let you and us sort the thing out. Tell 'em you, my sister, and me want flight clearance to Cuba, that we gotta parley there.

Actually, you'll be meetin' Castro and his chief of staff, General Juarez. It's to convince you that we're not playin' games. Me and Dolores will stay in Cuba. You and Juarez will get clearance to fly to D.C., in civvies. There you'll huddle with just one person, the secretary of defense. He wants to spill his guts to other people, that's his call. We're doin' our part to keep it as close to the vest as possible."

"What about Amy?" McNeill asked.

"She stays here until it's a done deal. Insurance. We know you won't risk her life, or let anyone else get trigger happy, because she'd be the first fall guy."

"You might also be prudent enough to tell your storm troopers," Takashi said, "that it would be sheer folly to try to issue gas masks to the civilian population. There aren't enough to go around, for one thing. For another, many of our chemicals can circumvent any gas mask made."

McNeill hugged Amy, said, "Keep the faith, honey," then walked through exits leading to the building exterior.

He held a white flag and was surprised to see that it was still very dark, that a light rain was falling, and that a southwest breeze was picking up.

"Over here," a voice called to him from behind an armored vehicle some fifty yards away.

"Hello, John, we've missed you," Deputy FBI Director William Turnbull greeted, as he stepped from behind the vehicle.

"Hi, Bill," McNeill responded. "Good thing I didn't get antsy in there. Without knowing you were out here, it's possible I could've detonated bombs I planted all along one side of the building and up there on that hill, where there's a mix for mustard gas. Most of you wouldn't have known what hit you. With this wind and rain, the soup would've headed mostly for a barren stretch of Canada."

"Jesus," Turnbull shuddered. "Why'd you hold off?"

"My daughter, for one," McNeill replied. "They've got her. We could've chanced it, but it would've been very iffy. Or, I could've used one of these ballpoint pens that can kill a man at fifty paces. Even if I were lucky enough to squeeze by that wrinkle, we'd still be in a pretty horrible corner."

"How so?" Turnbull asked. "We collared all their airplanes and impounded their materials. The pilots and ground crews played dumb, but I believe they really don't know what's up. We're doing chemical analysis on some of the barrels we seized. Some of them are undoubtedly mislabeled but it won't take long to get a handle on it."

"I was told not to get into specifics," McNeill said. "I can tell you this, though, you haven't neutralized all their planes and other potential for chaos, at least, that is, if what they've told me is true. They've stashed away some jets and remote-controlled rocket launchers. They also say they've got goons ready and able to spike water systems with colorless, odorless, undetectable poisons. Again, I have to buy what they're saying. They've convinced me they've been working on this plan for a long time. They've also got a mad-scientist genius and a pair of moxey CIA pros in their corner, to say nothing of Fidel Castro."

"Takashi, Bates and Urban," Turnbull observed.

"You got it," McNeill responded. "So, now the ball's in our court."

"Where do we lob it?" Turnbull asked.

"They, meaning a hood named Tomas Napoli, of Las Vegas fame, and his sister, Dolores Carto, want clearance to fly with me to Cuba in one of three jets they have hangared here. As part of my indoctrination on this whole business, I'm to meet with Castro and his chief military advisor to, allegedly, be told they're in the game for keeps. Then I'm to fly with the advisor to D.C. for a hush-hush huddle with the SecDef to spell out a list of demands I'm not at liberty to disclose to anybody else."

"They're crazy," Turnbull said. "They're provoking us to wipe Cuba off the face of the earth. It's just unthinkable we'd accept such bald-faced blackmail."

"I thought so, too," McNeill said, "until I considered the unimaginable. They push a few buttons and it's Judgment Day."

"Mutual self-destruction? Really that bad?"

"Could be. Would you want to chance that it isn't a possibility?"

"I'd sure hate to be the one to make that decision," Turnbull admitted.

"Here, take this," McNeill said, and handed over his detonator pen. "I've just disarmed what could've blown your boys up. I'll hang on to the other one, on the odd chance I might use it as a personal weapon.

"By the way," he added, "friend Takashi suggests we don't bother handing out oodles of gas masks. The supply's limited and his stuff can get around any defenses we might try."

"More good news," Turnbull said. "All right, we'll steal away like thieves in the night. You'll get your flight clearance. You'll have a fighter escort all the way to Cuba's air space. We wouldn't want anything untoward to happen to you or your new playmates. I'll have to alert my boss, of course, who will in turn brief the president. I'll pray it doesn't press a panic button. The top brass will have to take immediate security measures for themselves and their families. It'll be interesting to see how they can juggle their printed schedules and still keep the media types from sniffing out what's developing. Mother pin a rose on me."

"You know," McNeill said, "I'd kill all of them in a flash if it weren't for Amy. Clever bastards, they've got me right where they want me. The only thing I can do is play along. I can't even afford the tiny luxury of having the word passed back to her friends, just to mitigate a little bit of their worry."

"I was feeling sorry for myself, John," Turnbull said, grasping McNeill's shoulder. "But your bind makes me look like a piker. Keep the faith."

"That's what I told Amy."

# TWENTY-ONE

As Napoli and Dolores Carto made hurried, early morning arrangements to depart with McNeill for Cuba, Takashi Isoru approached Napoli in obvious agitation.

"I don't like this," Takashi said. "Why can't I come with you?" he shouted over the noise of the jet engines warming up.

"Somebody's gotta mind the shop," Napoli answered curtly. "You're a chemist, not a deal maker. You and Castro got nothin' to say to each other. That's why you, Carmine, Bates, and Urban are stayin' put. You got McNeill's kid as a hostage, the feds have pulled out, and we've got a foolproof back up. If anybody gets cute with us, we gas the country. What the hell more do you want?"

Takashi considered intently, then nodded and walked away.

Napoli signaled to Carmine Archangelo. The two conferred animatedly apart from the others. Bates and Urban looked on with studied indifference.

"Okay, let's do it," Napoli said, gesturing to his sister and McNeill to get into the jet.

McNeill smiled to himself as he compared outfits. Dolores wore a very feminine, flouncy yellow dress and matching pumps, a large white scarf wrapped loosely around her neck. Napoli looked very businesslike in a tan Armani, white-on-white shirt, dark blue tie, and Gucci alligators. McNeill wore his combat fatigues.

140

As soon as the camouflage curtain covering the hangar entrance was raised, the jet taxied forward and soon roared down the abbreviated runway, soaring in an incredibly sharp arc. McNeill had never experienced such a take-off.

When the plane leveled off, McNeill was impressed again, this time with the cabin's soundproofing. The engine's noise was barely perceptible. And the appointments were impeccable, as though they were in a posh clubhouse, curtains, seats, and carpeting color coordinated in white and beige pastels.

He looked across at Napoli and Dolores Carto and said, "We're going to have a fighter escort all the way to Cuba's air boundary."

Napoli seemed greatly surprised, then smiled as he reached for an intercom phone.

"That's right friendly of Uncle Sam," he said as he informed the pilot of the flight's impending company.

Within a moment, three air force jets appeared, two positioning themselves on either side of the plane, the other above it.

Napoli looked out the right-side porthole, smiled, and waved. The jet fighter pilot smiled and waved back.

"Good thing you told me about the escort," Napoli said. "If our pilot seen these guys suddenly appear without warnin', he probably woulda had a heart attack."

Addressing McNeill, Napoli said, "This book I'm holdin' is a hit list of places all across the U.S. that we can zap, one way or another. I'm gonna pick out one that's home to a lot of pigs. I'll have a message sent in the clear and, whamo, them little piggies ain't goin' to market. Castro will love it. He's convinced the CIA has killed a lot of his own pigs. Then there's the Bay of Pigs fiasco that made JFK look like a rank amateur."

"What if you're monitored and foiled?" McNeill asked.

"Like we been sayin', we ain't dummies. We send a few coded words. They're replayed eventually to an ad agency that don't know from nothin'. It turns around and tells certain radio stations to run a prearranged ad, say, a jingle. Our people are listenin' in. Next thing you know, there's a news story about some farmer's pigs gettin' overripe."

"This could be a set-up," McNeill said. "You could've picked a spot beforehand to make me think you really had a master plan."

"That's why I told you to pick a target and the dosage, deadly or non," Napoli replied easily. "You'd be our proof that we *can* telegraph the punches. If you don't cooperate, you could have some innocent lives on your conscience. Wanna play our pin the tail on the donkey? You can even call a local news department and confirm the hit even before it gets on the wires."

"All right, you win," McNeill answered. "Just give me the option of selecting a place for non-toxic, minimal impact."

Napoli thumbed quickly through his directory.

"Here," he said, "pick anything on this page," as he handed the book to McNeill.

McNeill closed his eyes and stabbed an index finger on the page.

Napoli noted the line, chuckled, and said, "Never thought I'd see you squeamish about knockin' out a few farm animals."

"Ever since Agent Orange, Napoli, ever since Agent Orange," McNeill responded with a hard edge to his voice.

He looked down through a sky that had cleared gloriously, shook his head, and inquired sadly, "How can you do what you're doing? How can you possibly justify ruining that land and its people?"

Dolores Carto studied the same view and said, "Oh, beautiful for spacious skies . . . purple mountains majesty . . . from sea to shining sea? Very touching, Colonel," she noted without rancor, even with a touch of sadness.

"To me," she continued, "Cuba has much the same appeal—and concern, only our weather is much more uniformly and consistently beautiful. My brother Tomas has interests that go beyond my sense of patriotism. Still, his basic motivation is, to me, understandable. He wants wealth and power to protect himself and his family and colleagues from all the predators who inhabit this merciless world. The meek inherit nothing.

"For years," she continued, "the United States supported Juan Batista as Cuba's president, one of the most corrupt rulers who ever lived. With U.S. interests and bribes, he sold my country down the river, turning Havana into a huge brothel with gaming tables."

"You think your brother's a choir boy," McNeill asked, "who has too many scruples to turn the clock back to the good old rackets days?"

"He's much too sophisticated and has much too great an appreciation for enlightened self-interest to kill the golden goose by inviting another revolution. A la Las Vegas, fools are invited, not coerced, to throw their money away, while they're provided with world-class entertainment and plush accommodations. And just look how many fools there are to be accommodated in the U.S.! They can't create lotteries, casinos, and riverboat gambling fast enough."

Instead of landing at Havana, as McNeill had expected, the jet continued, no longer with escort, south to a coastal mansion with a private jet strip.

McNeill looked down on a pink, cliff-edge stucco home he estimated would encompass fifteen thousand square feet of living space. It was gorgeous, lined with stately palms and multi-colored gardens.

As the jet touched down smoothly and taxied on a pink-colored tarmac toward a pink hangar, a ground crew clad in white overalls scampered to align a stairway for the passengers to alight, as a pink stretch limousine pulled into view.

The trio was driven expeditiously up a winding, pink-cobbled road to the cliff's summit.

There, awaiting them on an immense patio dotted with lounge chairs and umbrellaed tables, was Fidel Castro, grinning broadly, in a very casual white jump suit, bare feet in leather sandals, with his ubiquitous cigar.

At his side was a somber General Juan Juarez, in an open neck white military shirt, and white trousers and shoes.

"Buenas dias," Castro greeted as he stepped forward to embrace and kiss the cheeks of Dolores and Napoli.

McNeill's quick survey detected at least a half dozen guards with automatic weapons dispersed around the patio's fringe.

"Colonel McNeill," Castro said, extending his hand, "I've heard much about you and have been looking forward to meeting with you."

McNeill shook hands, said "Sir," and nodded curtly to Juarez, who responded in kind.

"Well, now," Castro said expansively, "let's sit and share a beverage, and have our little chat. Cigar, Colonel?"

When they were seated, Castro eyed McNeill, who had declined the cigar and said, "You have very impressive credentials. Scholar, renowned authority on chemical warfare, much-decorated hero, and a life of service in an elite corps.

"From that perspective," Castro continued, "I'd have to bet you've been racking your brain to find a way to throw a monkey wrench into our works. Right?"

"Yes," McNeill replied.

"Any luck?" Castro teased good-naturedly.

"Not yet, but hope springs eternal. You know, the old chestnut about the plans of mice and men."

Castro shrugged, grinned widely through his bushy beard and said, "My opponents have been trying to make my plans go astray for decades."

"Like the missile crisis?" McNeill asked with a mischievous smile.

Castro's grin froze.

"Touché, Colonel," he said, "but also like the Bay of Pigs. In any event, the operative word for my tenure is that of survival. And I've survived because I've spurned intimidation and have dared to thumb my nose at the Great Colossus. Now, I'm in the process of securing my country's future. This is to assure you, unequivocally, that I'm going to see our current project through to its ultimate conclusion, come what may."

# TWENTY-TWO

"From now on, you wanna see me, you come to me. I ain't your flunky," Carmine Archangelo announced as he entered the sparse office immediately adjacent to Takashi Isoru's, and which was shared by Corbin Bates and Carter Urban.

Archangelo looked around the room with unconcealed disdain. There were two heavy metal desks and swivel chairs, two stuffed chairs and a couch flanking a glass-top coffee table, several green shade lamps, light-green painted walls, dark-green carpeting, and no decorations, paintings, or pictures.

"Where'd ya find this dump, in a monastery?" Archangelo asked and added, "Waddaya want? I was just goin' to eat, and there's a race I wanna catch."

Urban was half-seated at one of the desks, behind which sat Bates.

"Aw, come on, Carmine," Bates said in a friendly manner, "we don't consider you anybody's go-fer. We just have to clear up a couple of points. Only take a minute."

As he was speaking, Urban walked toward Archangelo with an inviting smile, offered his hand, and said, "Good to see you, partner."

Archangelo took the proferred hand and instantaneously found his own being turned sharply to the left as Urban twisted the arm and pulled forward, using his victim's bulk to catapult him in a circle and flatten him with a loud thud to the floor.

Lying in pain, Archangelo reached for his tortured shoulder and was about to utter something when Urban bent down and gave him a vicious swipe at the temple with the knife edge of his hand. He lay still as a fallen giant oak.

"Get his coat off," Bates ordered, "then we'll drag him near enough to a desk so you'll be able to cuff one wrist and anchor it to a desk leg. It'll keep him from prowling around for a while after he comes to."

That task accomplished, Bates said, "On to step two."

Urban went to a desk drawer, removed a small black case, opened it, and took out a syringe, a rubber-topped vial containing clear fluid, and a plastic wrapped needle.

Expertly, he unwrapped the needle, attached it and wiped it with a cotton ball saturated with alcohol, inserted it into the vial, and extracted all the fluid. He held the hypodermic syringe vertically and pushed the plunger slightly, just enough to force a few drops of the fluid to spurt into the air.

He took another alcohol-soaked cotton ball, washed an area at Archangelo's tricep, and injected the needle, draining the contents of the vial.

"I know it's good stuff," Bates said, "but I've never seen it used on this big an ox."

"No problem,' Urban said, "I gave him enough to make even King Kong chirp like a canary. Think he's really been cut in on what Napoli knows?"

"Maybe not all, but certainly the lion's share of it," Bates answered. "Napoli's no dunce. He wants back-up in case the feds throw caution out the window and collar him. Jumbo here is his *consigliore*, his top gun. If nothing else, he'll know the soldiers who'll be assigned to spike water-works and the like. There's simply too much at stake for Napoli to keep everything to himself. Sure, it's strictly on a need-to-know basis. But the mob despises botched jobs.

It's zero tolerance for goombahs. For us, it could get down to fitting together pieces of a puzzle."

"Well," Urban said, "it won't take more than a few minutes to find out whether pal Tommy really left us in the dark to twist in the wind. He might try to look out for Archangelo, but I don't think he gives a second thought to what'd happen to you and me."

"Amen, brother," Bates said. "You pump the lump. I'll be back shortly."

Bates walked down the hall to the next office door and entered without knocking.

Takashi Isoru was being served tea by Akita, both of whom wore kimonos.

Takashi looked up with a meaningful scowl.

"It is discourteous to enter one's private abode without knocking and being admitted," Takashi said acerbically.

"Furthermore," he continued, "you do me the disrespect of not having removed your street shoes."

Before he could continue, Bates interrupted.

"Oh, can it, Rising Sun," Bates said, "I haven't got time for your contrived niceties. I'm in a hurry."

"For what?" Takashi asked, not irritably, but with a hint of apprehension.

"I'm here to tell you that Urban and I are leaving within the hour. If you have any brains in that sloped head of yours, you'll bug out, too."

Takashi appeared stunned.

"Why?" he asked, incredulously, waving Akita to leave their presence.

"We're no longer surrounded by an army of snoopers," he continued. "That demonstrates our credibility. We have the McNeill girl held hostage. We've proven that we pose a terrifying threat. Where is the worry, the concern?"

"Have you considered what happens if anything goes amiss with Napoli?" Bates asked sharply. "He's beyond our sight or sound. Suppose, for whatever reason or reasons, he suddenly gets cold feet and decides to take it on the lam. Without him, we're like sitting ducks. Puppets with nobody to pull the strings. We have no tunes to call. Any other analogies?"

Takashi gave a smile of superiority.

"I haven't been made privy to all Napoli's secrets," he said, "but I've been shown enough to retain a more than formidable defensive posture in terms of my own vulnerability.

"That is to say," he continued, "I can initiate coded attacks by way of the plan's airplanes and rocket launchers. Admittedly, this excludes individual mob hit men. But they only serve to gild the lily."

"I find that very hard to believe," Bates said, emphasizing his skepticism with an arched eyebrow.

"Akita," Takashi called, "bring me the black book with the dragon seal."

When she delivered it, Takashi again waved her away and said, "This directory reveals the locations and action code signals for six jet aircraft and fifty rocket launchers, the latter targeted for the fifty largest metropolitan areas in the United States."

Bates examined the little book and noted quickly that, as should always be the case, the codes were accompanied by counter codes to abort a mission.

"How do you know this book is legitimate?" Bates asked, as he handed it back. "Napoli could've given you a placebo instead of the real medicine."

Takashi smiled smugly as he poured himself another cup of steaming hot tea.

"You of all people should know how thorough and careful I am," he said. "I checked every single activating code and its abort. Each worked to perfection. Incidentally, the checks are recorded automatically by the recipient station. Napoli told me this was the case when he allowed that I should conduct a review at least twice a day. He, also, is a model of caution.

"That aside," Takashi continued, his naturally narrow eye lids fused into mere slits, "your sudden, impertinent behavior implies an inexplicable negligence to appreciate our relative positions."

"That's rich." Bates laughed. "Do you actually believe you had Urban and me boxed in like a pair of trained squirrels? Sure, you figured CIA stood for Central Incompetence Agency, right? You dangle your incriminating tapes and transcripts, and we just run ever faster on your treadmill.

"Look, you conceited little putz, the Company is always being caught with its pants down. If isn't the embarrassment of a mole one day, it's a traitor the next. It runs the gamut of flubbed assassinations to discredit to false analyses that cost lives and fortunes. Predictably, the CIA always stonewalls, declining comment. If the heat's hot enough, a congressional committee might get in on the fun. Behind closed-door hearings are held. Some congressmen get to strut their stuff, mostly to impress the yokels back home. Time passes. Appropriations are determined. The Company still comes away with tens of billions of dollars a year, mostly uncontrolled outside the agency. Why? The country's obsessed with spooks, real and imagined.

"So, shorty, we strung along with you not because of your worthless taped diaries but because it seemed an opportune thing to do. We rode together on an exciting merry-go-round. Only, on the last swing, you missed the brass ring. For you, the ride's over. Sayonara."

150

Bates pulled a silencer pistol from a chest holster and fired twice into Takashi's brow, exploding the back of his head.

He picked up the black book and left.

When Bates returned to his office, he found Urban listening with earphones to a tape recorder, scribbling rapidly.

"How'd we do?" he asked.

Urban smiled widely, held up a thumb and forefinger to form an O.

"Be with you in a minute," he said, and continued with his note-taking.

Bates looked at the prostrate Archangelo, whose slack-jawed, glassy-eyed gaze indicated he was nowhere near the ball park.

Urban put down his pen, clicked off the recorder, and flashed a sheet of paper.

"How many?" Bates asked.

"An even dozen. Murderers' Row, all in Vegas," Urban replied.

"Complete list?"

"Gotta believe," Urban said. "With the stuff I pumped into him, old Carmine would've ratted on his sainted mother. How about you?"

Bates tossed Urban the black book.

"Planes, rockets, and their locations," he said. "Takashi claimed he used Napoli's authorization to check the codes and their aborts, twice a day. Worked like a charm."

"Bingo!" Urban exclaimed. "Taki-san coughs up two-thirds of the riddle, Carmine the other third. That's one hundred percent on anybody's abacus. How'd you part with our Nip buddy?"

"If they do it right, he could provide a couple days' worth of food for his carp."

"What do we do with Carmine?"

"He's resting peacefully," Bates answered. "Let's just leave him here and allow nature to takes its course."

"What about the girl?"

"You take care of her," Bates said. "While you're doing that, I'm going to make myself into an instant hero by passing the word that everybody has the rest of the day off, everybody, that is, who didn't vanish after the feds pulled away."

"That include the kid's trusty?"

"Why not," Bates said. "She's just a luckless bird brain trying to hold onto a job nobody but her type would be willing to accept. A girl's got to eat."

"Generous to a fault."

Urban knocked at Amy's door. Gretel answered and, identifying the caller, stepped aside to admit him.

"You're released for the day, Miss Hauptman," he said, and added, "Please leave as soon as possible."

She was out in a flash and with a confused smile.

Amy's expression indicated a fear of some sort of abusive assault.

"She hadn't finished cleaning and straightening the place," Amy protested meekly.

"Not to worry, Miss McNeill," Urban tried to assure her. "You're leaving this place and won't be coming back. Gather up whatever you want and we'll take it with us."

Amy examined her outfit: designer jeans, frilly all-cotton white blouse, white moccasins.

"I don't want anything more than what I'm wearing," she said and added, "Where we going?"

Urban advanced toward her. She shuddered as he reached out, only to see him extract from her blouse pocket the ball-point pen her father had given to her.

He sat in a chair, pulled the pen apart, and began manipulating several serrated wheels within the body of the pen.

"What're you doing?" Amy asked, fear in her voice.

"Oh, just making a few minor adjustments," said Urban, smiling.

"There," he said, "all done. Let's be on our merry way."

Amy followed him out through the rear exit and was at once startled and cheered by the bright sunlight.

Urban led the way to a parking lot, which now contained only one vehicle, Urban's, a Nissan sport utility.

He opened the driver's side door and said, "Get in, Miss McNeill."

Amy hesitated, wondering desperately if she should make a run for it. She was fast, she knew, and could probably find cover in the dense surrounding foliage.

Urban seemingly fathomed her thoughts.

"If you run," he said wearily, "it'll only serve to postpone for a little while the inevitable. Please get in."

Amy sighed and obeyed.

Urban started the engine, punched the trip odometer, and they drove away.

After carefully monitoring the distance traveled, Urban stopped the vehicle, pulled the pen from his pocket, and made a final inspection.

"Do you like fireworks?" he asked.

Amy's blue eyes widened, but she was speechless.

Urban depressed the top of the pen. There was an immediate succession of tremendous explosions. It was such a frightening surprise that she couldn't reconcile how many blasts there were. Two, three?

"Did you blow up the chemical dump outside the building?" Amy asked.

"No," Urban answered, "that's why I played with your daddy's detonator. It's all a matter of manipulating the codes. No point in gassing the good citizens of Montana. Hang on, we're getting away from here in quick time."

# TWENTY-THREE

"You know, Colonel, you really ought to change into something more appropriate for the upcoming occasion," Fidel Castro said to McNeill as they breakfasted on El Presidente's patio with Napoli, General Juarez, and Dolores Carto.

"Coming from someone who has made fatigues a fashion statement, that strikes me as downright funny," McNeill tweaked.

Castro, dressed in jungle fatigues, joined in laughing at the paradox as well as McNeill's impertinence.

"I know, I know," Castro said, "I'm preaching don't do like I do, do like I say, but I wouldn't want Washington to think my hospitality was anything less than gracious."

"Very well," McNeill shrugged, "I'll accept your offer to make myself more presentable. We'll chalk it up to my appreciation for being served a couple of great meals without being shot in the back of the head."

McNeill excused himself, went to his luxurious suite, and exchanged his camouflage field uniform for a very expensive light-blue Panama suit, white-on-white shirt, dark blue tie, and matching blue shoes. Everything fit to perfection. As he dressed, he felt somewhat guilty in relishing sips of the strong Cuban coffee that had been brought to his room.

While he was gone, Napoli said, "I been readin' up on the history of Legionnaires' Disease. Saw it in one of the weekly magazines. Interestin'. It took the medical pros a near eternity to trace the source of mold vapors that were pumped out through air-conditionin' ducts. Killed or flattened a lot of geezers before they finally put a finger on the culprit. Got me to thinkin'. It'd be easy to slip some of our chemical slugs into an air-conditionin' system."

"Tomas," Dolores Carto said, half-smiling, "the workings of your devious mind are wonders to behold."

"Why not?" General Juarez asked approvingly. "It fits with the old adage that knife fighters don't have rules."

Castro reacted noncommitally, content to puff on his cigar.

A white-frocked servant came to Castro's side and deferentially placed a fax sheet on the table in front of him.

Castro scanned it quickly, smiled, and handed it to Juarez, who in turn passed it to Napoli.

It contained a copy of the front-page summary portion of *The Wall Street Journal*, with today's date, which reported that authorities were investigating a feared outbreak of hoof-and-mouth disease among pigs in Fitchton, Nebraska, forty miles south of Lincoln. Readers were referred to a two-paragraph item on page twenty.

"Short and sweet," Napoli said. "It happened too soon for fuller coverage. That'll come tomorrow. Serves our purpose. McNeill knows where we'd hit and what. Here he comes."

"My, what a splendid difference," Dolores said.

"Thank you, and allow me to return the compliment," McNeill replied, as he scanned her low-cut, ultra-fashionable gold lamé cocktail dress.

"You'll be interested in this," Napoli said as he handed McNeill the fax.

McNeill frowned then asked, "Did you use industrial strength or a simulant?"

"Let's wait and see," Napoli teased mischievously. "You can get filled in when we get to D.C. My sister and I decided to go with you and the general. At first, I thought we'd sit tight here. But, what the hell, I wanna be on hand to pop the champagne corks. Man, it's gonna be better'n breakin' the bank at Monte Carlo. While I'm sackin' out, Dolores can check the garage sales and scoop up anything her heart desires. Ready, everybody?"

They all stood. Castro shook hands with Juarez, Napoli, and Dolores, and said, "Hasta la vista."

When he offered his hand to McNeill, the latter, grim faced, turned about and walked toward the awaiting limousine.

"I didn't take him to be a poor loser," Castro said.

"What do you expect from a Yankee?" Juarez asked rhetorically.

Moments after their jet took off, Napoli saw in the distance the approach of three U.S. fighter aircraft that would be aligning with them as soon as they passed Cuba's air corridor.

"Good," he said, clapping his hands. "They'll be all ready for us. No hassle at customs. We'll breeze through traffic in limos, probably with motorcycle escorts. You guys'll go to the Pentagon, Dolores and me'll go to the Madison. What a day!"

"What do you know," McNeill said, "those are marine fighters. Maybe the situation's well in hand after all."

Napoli, unamused, reached for his phone, punched in some numbers, and waited. He slammed the phone down furiously.

"What?" Juarez inquired.

"Still can't get through to LibertyAire in Kalispel. Lines're screwed up. 'Undetermined cause' they keep sayin'. 'Please be patient," they keep sayin'. Shoulda been somethin' about it on the news."

"Our people weren't told to look for reports out of Montana, only Nebraska," Juarez said.

"Relax," he continued, "I'm sure it's only a technical inconvenience."

Johnny Liconi was arm-in-arming it with his bottle-blonde girlfriend in front of Las Vegas's Riviera Hotel when they were suddenly confronted by five men in conservative business suits.

All five drew pistols. One flashed an I.D. and badge and shouted, "FBI, you're under arrest."

Two others gruffly grabbed Liconi, another hand-cuffed him, while still another frisked him.

The bottle-blonde hustled away, gasping, as she heard a phrase she'd encountered in countless TV police dramas, "You have a right to remain silent. . . ."

In less than an hour, the scene was repeated eleven times within the Las Vegas corporate limits.

One hundred fifty FBI special agents had vacuumed a dirty dozen with warrants and the stunning charge of conspiring to injure the persons and property of citizens of the United States of America.

In a private hangar at Detroit International Airport, FBI Special Agent Sam Tucker and two associates appeared suddenly in front of pilot Bill Gateman.

Tucker displayed his identification and announced, "FBI. We have a warrant to impound this aircraft and all equipment in this hangar. You can lower your hands, mister; you are not under arrest and are free to leave."

Similar confrontations occurred in private hangars at airports in New York, Washington, D.C., Atlanta, Chicago, and Los Angeles.

"You are right, as usual, Tomas," Dolores Carto said after their jet touched down at Dulles International.

Waiting outside were two stretch limousines and eight motorcycles with helmeted police officers.

As Napoli and company descended on the portable stairway, a tight-lipped official wordlessly directed Napoli and Dolores to one vehicle, and McNeill and Juarez to the other.

One set off, sirens blaring, for the Pentagon. The other was escorted, without sirens, to the Madison Hotel.

"They're uptight as hell," Napoli said to Dolores. "That's good. That's very good."

When they were in their impeccable suits, Napoli turned on the large television, referred to a guide, clicked to CNN Headline News, and fixed drinks for Dolores and himself.

With an ear to the TV sound, he glanced around approvingly at the accommodations.

Before he'd finished his critical appraisal, he swirled quickly to watch as well as hear the news anchor announce, "Hundreds of firefighters battle a square-mile blaze in dry forests near Kalispel, in far northwest Montana." (A background map appeared outlining Montana and a portion of British Columbia, with an arrow zooming in to pinpoint Kalispel.)

The scene cut to a tired, blackened face, with the lower one-third superimposed identification: Firefighter Lowell Madrigal, who related, "People said they heard one or more big explosions. Could've been a plane crash, for all we know."

The scene cut to an on-the-scene reporter and pulled back to reveal flames leaping fifty and more feet into the air.

"Except for a recent and light rainfall, the area's been parched," the reporter said. "Among other things, the initial blast knocked out local phone communications, which are expected to resume service within hours. The blaze, which is under arson investigation, could take days to bring under control. For CNN Headline News, I'm—"

Napoli clicked off the TV, looked at his sister, and glowered.

# TWENTY-FOUR

As the limo came within a mile of the Pentagon, the four motorcycle escorts turned off their sirens and flashing lights and departed.

"We're not there yet," Juarez noted, puzzled by the sudden disappearance of their escort.

"Probably don't want to raise any media eyebrows," McNeill said. "We'll no doubt get out at some obscure entrance. There are always reporters hanging around to see if anything out of the ordinary is in the works. We're definitely out of the ordinary. They can't chance it that some eagle eye might spot you."

Juarez smiled in agreement and said, "You seem to know their mind set, Colonel. I'm sure they want to keep the purpose of our visit under tight wraps."

They were deposited at the entrance to a loading ramp, after which the limousine drove out of view to a remote parking lot.

Two tall marine sergeants under arms stepped forward, snapped to attention, and saluted McNeill.

McNeill nodded and said "Good afternoon, Sergeants."

Behind the guards, a short, beetle-browed army major general got out of a battery-powered tram. The name badge on his blouse identified him as Justin Calloway.

"Get in," he said, pointing at the eight-passenger vehicle, "we're taking you to the secretary of defense."

McNeill and Juarez sat behind the driver and major general and in front of the two marine noncoms.

They sped almost noiselessly along seeming miles of busy corridors, past hordes of occupants who paid them not the slightest heed.

The tram stopped at a ponderous door labeled "Q Clearance Personnel ONLY."

Juarez looked questioningly at McNeill.

"The most secret of top secret," McNeill answered.

One of the marine sergeants pressed a doorbell button. There was a clicking sound. He opened the door, stepped aside to admit McNeill and Juarez, then closed the door behind them.

Inside the enormous windowless room was a comparably huge, rectangular conference table, at the head of which was a man in civilian attire. Behind him was a floor-to-ceiling multicolor map of the world that covered an entire wall. Four armed marines were positioned at each of the four corners, hands on open holsters.

The civilian at the head of the table stood and said, "I am the secretary of defense. The gentlemen to my right are our military chiefs of staff. Please be seated to my left."

No names, no ranks, no greeting. Only the chilliest reception since the beginning of the Ice Age.

McNeill suddenly felt the need to wipe his brow as he sat and glanced at the bemedaled senior officers across the table. Solid stone world-class poker faces that would make those on Mount Rushmore look positively animated.

Juarez went to his chair but remained standing.

Without invitation, he said, grandly, "Gentlemen, I believe we can expedite matters by having Colonel McNeill give you a thorough, expert appraisal of my nation's military capabilities, vis-à-vis the United States. As he will relate, in-field demonstrations of our potential have been made for the colonel's evaluation. Furthermore, he last met as late as this morning with President Castro and can acquaint you accurately with Cuba's posture from the highest level."

McNeill waited respectfully for a question or signal.

A red phone near the defense secretary rang. He picked up the receiver, listened stoically for several seconds, and said, "Send them in."

Two civilian men and a young woman entered.

McNeill was dumbstruck.

"Amy!" he screamed and ran toward his daughter.

"Dad!" she screamed back, and rushed toward him.

He picked her up and twirled around several times, consumed by a choking, sobbing spasm of total surprise, joy, and relief.

Of the onlookers, only General Juarez appeared other than pleased. He was totally baffled.

A hand tried the doorknob and found it locked. Another hand, that of a bellhop, inserted a key, turned the knob, and withdrew.

The door was opened an inch, soundlessly, then a foot kicked it wide open.

Ten men burst into the top floor suite of the Madison Hotel and leveled pistols at the startled occupants.

The lead intruder shouted, "FBI! Tomas Napoli and Dolores Napoli Carto, you're under arrest."

"Amy, honey, how—?" McNeill sputtered as he tried to comprehend the incredible development.

Amy looked at the men beside her, smiled, and shrugged her shoulders, as if to indicate she was overwhelmed, also.

Until that moment, the pair flanking his daughter had been inconsequential blurs.

"Nice to see you again, Colonel," Corbin Bates said.

"Likewise," the other added. It was Carter Urban.

McNeill took Amy's hand and stepped, weak kneed, two paces back, and stared in open-mouthed, blank-eyed wonder.

The red phone rang again. The secretary of defense listened for ten seconds and replaced the receiver without comment.

"Gentlemen, Miss McNeill, please join us," he said, and added, "Bates?"

Bates remained standing by a chair and replied, "The fat lady has sung, Mister Secretary. The show's over."

"Thank you," the secretary said and turned to the still-standing General Juarez.

"That call I received a moment ago advised that Napoli and Carto have been arrested."

Juarez slumped to his chair with a pallor that suggested he was a candidate for cardiac arrest.

"It's also been confirmed to my complete satisfaction," the secretary continued, "that every last one of your chemical-warfare tricks has been neutralized. So much so that even the one programmed for today was aborted. You are now a toothless ambassador without portfolio. You have two hours to leave the country."

When they were outside the conference room, McNeill addressed Bates and said, "You sure had me finessed. I pegged you two as a pair of Darth Vaders."

"Actually, we are," Bates acknowledged. "It's just that we retain a smidgeon of redeeming social value."

"Whatever you are," McNeill said, "thanks for saving Amy, to say nothing of the country."

"We had plenty of help, yours included," Bates said.

"What about Takashi?" McNeill asked.

"When I solicited him for a contribution to our widows and orphans fund, he got a migraine even a bucket of Tylenol couldn't relieve," Bates deadpanned.

"Archangelo?"

"Carmine," Urban answered, "contradicted the axiom that you can't be in more than one place at the same time. He is now all over various parts of northwest Montana."

"Gretel Hauptman?"

"They let her go, Dad," Amy interrupted. "I'm sort of glad, although I hated her at the time. She was just sort of caught up in the whole thing, trying to make a living when she probably couldn't land anything else."

"What happens to Napoli, his sister, his hoods, and Castro?" McNeill asked.

"Don't know yet," Bates said. "Depends on what the president, state, and defense want to do. It's dicey. Trials and a protest to the U.N. might reveal more than we want to reveal, for national security purposes. On the other hand, it wouldn't seem right to simply let them off the hook, from a practical, not legalistic, standpoint. What're you going to do?"

McNeill put an arm around Amy and said, "Goin' fishin,' and doing a lot of other things together that I let slip by in the past."

"We'll keep in touch, McNeill," Bates said, "We'll need you the next time the chemical genie sneaks out of the bottle."

"Next time!"

"Count on it, pal."